THE GUARDIANS OF ISRAEL

JOHN M. COYLE

Order this book online at www.trafford.com
or email orders@trafford.com

Most Trafford titles are also available at major online book retailers.

Print information available on the last page.

ISBN: 978-1-4907-9986-5 (sc)
ISBN: 978-1-4907-9988-9 (hc)
ISBN: 978-1-4907-9987-2 (e)

Library of Congress Control Number: 2020903638

Trafford rev. 02/21/2020

www.trafford.com
North America & international
toll-free: 1 888 232 4444 (USA & Canada)
fax: 812 355 4082

CHAPTER I

Recess

I T WAS 12 O'CLOCK THAT FRIDAY AFTERNOON, AND THE courthouse in Eureka, California had just broken for lunch recess. This was the last in a series of trials regarding the criminal enterprise led by William Edward Masey, Esq. Detective William Sullivan had been crisscrossing the country. For the past year testifying against the group that for nearly 5 years had kidnapped expectant mothers in order to steal their unborn children for the purpose of brokering the children to wealthy clients of Masey.

Thus far, the group of William Masey, Jake Millosovich, Samone, the prostitute, Jim Haskel and Randy Anderson had amassed death sentences and two life terms. The Eureka, California matter was a death penalty case as well, but not yet completed.

The "Butcher" doctor, Mordechai Wasserman, decided he did not want to be executed, so he chose to cooperate and provide states evidence against the other co-defendants. Sully, who had finished testifying Monday morning, had remained to assist the prosecutors with their direct examination of Doctor Wasserman. The doctor had been testifying for almost four full days now.

During Friday morning's testimony, the doctor related that after he had performed the c-section on Peggy Anderson, he tended to the care of the baby girl. He testified that when the infant was secure and sleeping, he went into an adjoining room and cracked open a bottle of Johnny Walker Black Label. The doctor related as he sat sipping on the scotch that he had heard horrifying screams coming from the makeshift surgery room.

Wasserman testified, "I went into the O.R. and witnessed the horror of Randy Anderson sodomizing the victim. She was screaming like I had never heard before. She resisted violently, but the more she struggled, the more aroused Randy became. The blood was rushing from the still open incision in her belly."

The doctor admitted that he left the room doing nothing or saying anything to dissuade Randy.

Wasserman stated, "She bled to death, Peggy Anderson, her struggling forced the blood to gush out of her and she was gone. I guess Randy was done as well, because he walked outside and lit up a joint. He sat out there on the porch and smoked his weed, savoring the moment of his latest conquest."

Doc. Wasserman had provided testimony in each case that detailed how the group operated. Jake Mellosovich, with the help of Samone, would locate the potential targets. The group of Jake, Samone, Jim and Randy would conduct surveillance of the targeted woman and gather background intelligence. A member of the group would break into the medical offices overseeing the woman's pregnancy and obtain her medical records. Jake would deliver all of the data to the attorney, William Masey, who would then make the final call (whether or not to take her.)

The "Butcher" also provided Detectives with the locations used by him to conduct the procedures of removing the babies from their mother's womb.

In some instances, the doctor knew where the victim's mothers were actually buried. In those cases, in which he did not know the actual grave site, Investigators were able to locate the makeshift graves using cadaver dogs. These gravesites were generally within 20 yards of the structure used by the doctor to perform the c-sections on the victim mothers.

Sully walked out of the courthouse. He was exhausted, but, felt confident that this case would go to the jury by the end of the day. The Doc had undergone cross-examination for the last hour and a half. Sully noted that in the previous trials, the Defense attorneys in an effort to either discredit or confuse the Doctor, usually ended up extracting even more damaging testimony, crippling any hope that they may have had for their clients.

Sully sat down on one of the granite steps. He leaned back against a Parthenon like column and lit one of his favorite cigars. It was a Tranquito from Leon's Cigars. Leon's was a hole-in-the-wall cigar shop at Sixth Street and Western Avenue in Los Angeles. The Cuban immigrants tolled daily hand-rolling a fine blend of seven tobaccos. To Sully, this was a Cuban cigar!

Sully relaxed puffing on this smoke as people passed by. Most smiled and nodded with approval of the alluring aroma. Oh, there were one or two indignant leers, but Sully just grinned and continued to enjoy his Tranquito.

As Sully sat composed, he thought about his trip home at the end of the day. This weekend would be filled with celebration. Shawn Patrick Sullivan would be the honoree at his first birthday. Sully knew that Meg was putting together a party fit for a Member of the Royal Family of England! Sully felt bad that he could not help out with the planning or the preparation, however, he was confident that Meg's sister, Clara, and brother-in-law, Robert, would more than make up for his absence.

It was now 1:00 o'clock and Sully returned to the courtroom. The Defense continued to attack Doctor Wasserman with their cross-examination. Sully felt that the team of Defense attorneys knew beforehand that they were not going to shake his testimony. They were merely putting on a show for their clients, as well as the jury.

It was almost 2:30 p.m. when the Defense rested. The Judge stood and announced a fifteen-minute recess before the Deputy District Attorney would begin his re-direct of Doctor Wasserman. During the cross-exam, the Deputy District Attorney kept a keen eye on the jury looking for reactions to either questions posed by the Defense, or the answers given by Doctor Wasserman.

As the trial resumed, the District Attorney asked the Doctor only two follow-up questions. This was done to clear up issues that the Defense was attempting to cloud with confusion.

"Doctor Wasserman," asked the Deputy District Attorney, "You have testified that Peggy Anderson, who was eight and a half months pregnant, was kidnapped by Defendants Jake Millosovich, Samone Henry, Jim Haskel and Randy Anderson."

"You further testified that the victim was brought to you at 856 Claremont Street, an abandoned house, 3 miles east of Eureka, California."

"You have told this court that you performed a c-section surgical procedure on Mrs. Anderson, removing her unborn baby girl from its womb."

"Now, I ask you Sir."

"Did you, at that time, know why you were performing this surgical procedure?"

Doc Wasserman responded, "Yes Sir, I was securing the infant for William Edward Masey, Esq."

"My second question of you Sir is: Why did the Defendant known to this court as William Edward Massey want the child of Peggy Anderson?"

Doc Wasserman replied: "He was selling the baby to a client."

The Deputy District Attorney looked at the jury as if to say..." Does that clear it up for you?"

He then turned to the Judge and stated, "The People rest, your honor."

Sully noted that the time was 3:30 p.m. and thought to himself… Probably not enough time for closing arguments.

Just then, the Judge excused the jury for the remainder of the day. Once the jury was out of the courtroom the Judge informed both the Prosecution and the Defense team that they would have the weekend to prepare their closing arguments, which he would hear along with the jury on Monday morning.

The court then stood at recess for the weekend.

Sully smiled at the young Deputy District Attorney. They shook hands and Sully stated, "Nice job Counselor. You ready for closing arguments?"

Mark Campbell, the Deputy District Attorney was a graduate of Berkeley Law School. His first job was with a firm in San Francisco specializing in Criminal Law.

He found the group of Defense attorneys lacking in ethics. Although graduating from Berkeley, a University known for its Liberal, and in some cases, left-wing teachings, he shifted his pursuit to defending the victims of crime instead of those who prey on others.

Campbell grinned at Sully and stated, "Detective, I had my closing arguments prepared days before we started jury selection."

"These bastards are going to fry!"

Sully nodded with approval and said, "Well Sir, if you don't need me to be there at your table,

I think I'll forego the drive back up here."

Mark told Sully that he would not need him and at the same time, thanked him for his assistance during the trial.

As Sully began to walk away, he turned and asked, "Say, maybe you can fax me a copy of your closing next week."

Mark Campbell responded, "Be glad to."

It was Saturday morning, and on the drive back to Los Angeles, Sully tried to count the number of days he had spent apart from Meg and young Shawn. It was way too many to count. With all the trials that Sully participated in regarding this case, well, it was just too overwhelming.

Sully then had another thought flash into his memory. There was another three-day trip he had taken to Las Vegas.

And, although this trip was not related to the kidnappings and baby thefts, it was significant.

Sully and Officer Theodore Xavier Thomas took a side trip to Sin City to pay a birthday visit to Belinda Roberson. Belinda was the disgraced officer involved in the execution style murder of Jamal Jefferson; the young gang member turned police informant.

Belinda was spending her days and nights in a Nevada State Prison, just outside of Las Vegas. The visit had been arranged by Detective Rob Jamison of the Las Vegas Metro Police Department's Intelligence Unit.

Although Belinda, a Los Angeles Police Officer gone bad was involved in the murder of Jamal Jefferson, a crime which occurred in Los Angeles, she was never prosecuted by the Los Angeles Deputy District Attorney. In order to comprehend this, you would have to back date yourself just over a year ago. Sully discovered during his investigation of the Jamal Jefferson murder, that Officer Roberson was involved. He also found out that she herself had grown up as a gang member. A manhunt, or in this case, a woman hunt was then begun.

Roberson, it turned out was in Las Vegas with her boyfriend and fellow homicide suspect Mad Dog. The pair was in Las Vegas doing a drug deal for which they had been arrested and jailed, then came their daring escape, which left two Deputy Sheriff Officers dead.

In the pursuit that followed their escape, Mad Dog was killed in a horrific car crash. The crash left Officer Belinda Roberson paralyzed from the neck down.

The Los Angeles District Attorney did not feel that California's penal system was best suited for Belinda Roberson. After all, she killed two police officers in the state of Nevada. And so, Nevada should, after all, have dibs on Belinda.

Sully surmised that the District Attorney in Los Angeles felt that once Belinda Roberson was wheeled into a California courtroom in her paralyzed state, all the bleeding- heart liberals would flock to her side.

No, the District Attorney probably thought Nevada is the best place for "Sweet Belinda."

In order for the District Attorney to show empathy for Jamal Jefferson and his loved ones, he worked out a deal with the United States Attorney for the Central District of California.

The deal, in essence was this:

The U.S. Attorney's Office and the United States Department of Justice would prosecute Roberson for violating the civil rights of Jamal Jefferson. She had used her position as a police officer to identify Jamal Jefferson as a police informant, thus targeting him for an execution gang style.

The District Attorney was able to paint this as an assault under the color of authority, putting it in the hands of the Feds.

In this manner, the District Attorney could bring Belinda Roberson to justice for the murder of Jamal Jefferson and at the same time keep her in Nevada. After all, the Feds could try her in Nevada, as well as in California. And, it would actually be easier for the Justice Department to do so citing the hardship on the defendant by moving her under the conditions of her current medical needs.

At any rate, it was here in Nevada that Belinda Roberson would be spending her 28th birthday.

Well, actually, it would be her first of many birthdays.

Sully and Ted entered prison. Belinda was lying on her back, propped up slightly in an upright position. This enabled her to see not only the television, but anyone who walked in.

As Sully and Ted entered the room, they were carrying a small birthday cake with one lit candle. The pair was singing the Happy Birthday song to Belinda, though not always in tune.

Ted was first to speak. Wishing Belinda a Happy Birthday, Ted stated, "I know you're probably too physically fucked up. Oh, I mean physically challenged, to blow out your own candle. So, I'll do that for you."

Ted took a deep breath and blew out the lone candle. Ted cut the cake into three sections placing the pieces onto party plates that he and Sully had brought with them.

Ted gave the first piece to Belinda. Or, at least placed it on her bed tray next to her water container and straw. The straw at least was in reach of her mouth. The cake was close, but alas, poor Belinda did not have the use of her hands and arms, so the fork provided by Ted just stayed stuck in the cake. Ted handed Sully the second piece and kept the third section for himself.

Sully and Ted then began to eat the cake. They savored each bite. Sully and Ted both moaned while eating the Birthday cake. Anyone not knowing what was going on in Belinda's room might mistake the moans of cake delight for the groans of sexual ecstasy.

Ted and Sully finished their pieces of the cake and looked at Belinda. They stated simultaneously,

"That was really good cake!"

"What's the matter Belinda?"

"You haven't touched yours!"

The two smiled, wished Belinda a Happy Birthday and stated, "See you next year!"

As they began to exit. Sully noticed that the television was turned on. He hadn't noticed before because he could not hear it. Belinda had ear plugs on so she could listen, but anyone else in the room couldn't hear. Sully saw that the cable channel was playing a "Rap" song. Actually "Gangsta Rap."

Sully reached up and turned the set to the Lifetime Channel for Women and departed the room.

CHAPTER II

Happy Birthday Shawn

I T WAS EARLY SATURDAY EVENING WHEN SULLY arrived home. As he pulled his city car into the driveway, he could see that Robert had tended to the needs of the yard. The lawn was freshly mowed and edged. Sully thought that if he ever was to quit doing his own yard work and decided to hire a gardener, he would first review resumes of laid off aerospace engineers. Sully had not seen his yard this well groomed in several years.

Sully grabbed his bags out of the trunk of the car and walked into the house through the side door. Meg was standing in the kitchen at the oven. Meg had the oven door open, while stabbing a rump roast with a meat fork. Meg looked over her shoulder and gave Sully a seductive smile. Meg jerked the fork out of the meat and closed the oven. Meg ran over to greet Sully with a wanting kiss and the hug of a boa constrictor.

Meg stated, after a long tender kiss,

"The meat's done!"

Sully responded, "Mine is just beginning to sizzle!"

Meg giggled knowing exactly was Sully was alluding to.

Meg asked,

"Are you ready to eat?"

Sully smiled and answered,

"Oh yeah, more than you can imagine!"

Meg looked at Sully and said:

"Yeah, Yeah, I know what you have on your mind."

"I'll make you a deal. You sit down and we'll eat the dinner that I put my heart and soul into."

"And, after we have a nice quiet, romantic dinner, I'll let you decide what you want to eat for dessert!"

As Sully sat down at the table with Meg. He asked,

"Shawn sleeping?"

"No, Meg replied, "He is spending the night with his Aunt Lara and Uncle Robert."

Sully nodded, letting Meg know that he understood. Sully was careful not to eat too much. After all, he knew that Meg had planned a night of lovemaking. And, he did not want to overindulge himself at the dinner table. Sully noted that Meg had placed conservative portions on her plate as well.

After dinner Sully and Meg sat out on the patio with a glass of red wine. While the two sipped on the nectar of a California vineyard and held hands, ever so gently. They talked, mostly about Sully's most recent trip to Eureka, California and the Peggy Anderson murder trial.

Sully had never divulged any of the gruesome details of any of the kidnap-murder cases. Sully felt it the wiser choice to shield Meg from the hellish evil that had befallen the mothers-to-be. A fate she herself was slated for.

It was almost 9:00 o'clock when Sully and Meg entered the shower of their master bedroom. The Sullivan household shower could be described as a playpen big enough for four, but actually, just right for two people in love to lavish each other in a shower orgy. That is exactly what took place that Saturday night. Meg and Sully lathered each other with messaging like strokes, which blended with groping-like foreplay. The love starved couple frolicked in the shower for about twenty-five minutes before moving their lustful play into the bed.

After completely satisfying each other's needs, both Sully and Meg fell into a restful slumber while embracing each other in what is affectionately referred to as the "spooning position."

It was 8:30 a.m. Sunday morning when Sully awoke to the aroma of freshly ground coffee. Sully resisted his inner self's desire to stay in bed and begrudgingly rolled out of bed. Sully splashed some cold water on his face, removing any evidence of a visit from the sandman the night before. After brushing his teeth, visiting the toilet for a quick deposit, Sully donned a robe and went into the kitchen to enjoy a hot cup of coffee. Upon entering the kitchen Sully caught sight of Meg standing at the island counter. She was standing, in her bare feet, wearing a pink baby doll nighty. Sully thought to himself, Wow! Sully's mind then began to drift as he pondered the idea of morning sex.

After all, he thought to himself, the only thing better than a night concluded by intercourse, is a day begun by the same.

Sully put the thought of jumping Meg to rest when he saw that she was icing a birthday cake for wee little Shawn. Sully poured his coffee, and at the same time noted that Meg's cup was empty. Sully offered Meg a refill and a kiss, both of which she accepted. Sully took his coffee out to the patio and while sipping on the brew, took a walk around the backyard. Sully noted that the yard was party ready. Tables and chairs were all set up. The Bar-B-Que was clean, and the tank gauge read "Full."

Sully saw the helium tank and bag of balloons in the corner of the patio. Sully sighed with relief knowing that there was at least one job left for him to help with his son's birthday party.

The party was slated to kick off at 2:30 p.m., but it was 1:00 o'clock when Robert and Clara arrived with the guest of honor. Shawn had just awoken from his noon nap and Clara was readying him for a bath before decking him out in his new shirt and pants. Meg had laid out a white tee-shirt with green trim on the sleeves and neck. On the chest area of the shirt was a green shamrock.

At 2:00 o'clock, Sully had all the balloons inflated and tied in place. The beer for the adults was on ice and the fruit punch was chilled and waiting to stain the lips of the toddlers who would join in on the festivities. Fact be known, there really would not be that many kids at the party. Just a few of the nurses that Meg had worked with at the hospital and the associates he worked with at the Newton Street Division were invited. Sully's associates were all older like himself. Sully is the only one of the Detectives that had begun a family this late in his life.

Robert fired up the Bar-B-Que and began cooking the meat for the event, Pork ribs, beef tri-tip and Louisiana hot links. Complimenting the menu which included potato salad, cole slaw and fruit salad, were of course, bar-b-qued baked beans. It was 3:30 p.m. when the food was ready to be served.

The party was going well with the adults visiting with each other and the kids playing, all three of them. The two little boys at the party were both 5 years old and were very good with Shawn.

Sully grinned as they played hard like little boys do, but, at the same time, they were mindful of Shawn's age and treated him with care. Sully thought this showed an uncanny maturity of the youngsters.

Ralph Doyle entered the backyard, gave Sully a nod and Meg a big hug. Sully saw something in Ralph that puzzled him. Doyle seemed distant and predisposed.

Sully watched Doyle as he walked over to the cooler and grabbed a long neck. Sully thought to himself just how similar in appearance Doyle was to Gene Hackman. Not only were they physically similar, but their mannerisms were very much alike.

As the night wore on and after little Shawn opened his gifts and embedded his hand into the Birthday cake, the cigars began to fill the backyard with their aroma.

The drink of choice for the evening was split between long necks and Black coffee. For Doyle, it was a steady diet of long necks. A fact that began to concern Sully.

Sully watched for a moment as Doyle and Meg stood in the corner. They appeared to be engaged in deep conversation. Sully noted however that Doyle exhibited symptoms of intoxication. Sully knew instinctively that there was something seriously troubling his good friend.

Sully began to walk toward Meg and his pal. Meg saw Sully approach and waved him off. Sully redirected his steps and buddied up with Robert to finish his cigar and Silver Bullet.

Meg had detoured Sully because Ralph Doyle was opening up to her about things Doyle was not proud of. Meg knew that if Sully entered into the conversation, Doyle would clam up. Doyle had been telling Meg of his concern for an informant he had cultivated, and who was now missing. Doyle told Meg that the girl, Amanda Cavanaugh, a sweet Irish girl, had just celebrated her nineteenth birthday. Doyle described her as a sweet, but misguided teen.

Doyle related that Amanda had been led into a Neo-Nazi following by a boyfriend, but that she was smart enough to recognize the dangers associated with the Skinhead Movement. Doyle told Meg that it was a snap recruiting her to be a snitch. She just didn't believe in the ideology of the Skinheads and felt obligated to bring them down.

This is where it became interesting to Meg and about the point when she gave Sully the go away signal.

Doyle began to drift somewhat. Meg wasn't sure at first whether it was emotion or alcohol, but Doyle began what became a confession of sorts.

"She was almost innocent."

Doyle began.

"A beautiful wee lass. A full 5 feet, 6 inches tall. No more than 120 pounds. Light red hair and green eyes. Large breasts and a hard-flat stomach."

Doyle added,

"Before she wised up, she had Nazi SS lightening bolts tattooed on the back of her neck, and a small swastika tattoo just below her bikini line."

Meg interrupted.

"What? How do you know that?"

Doyle answered,

"It's hard not to notice it when you're down there having lunch!"

Meg knew that Doyle could see the expression of shock in her face. After all, although Meg was only a Reserve Officer, she knew that it was a major "No, no" to become personally involved with an informant.

Doyle read Meg right and said,

"Yeah, I know, I fucked up. But this girl just got to me. I couldn't help myself. And, the more involved we got, the more I wanted to be with her. Now she's missing and I can't help it but I think she's in trouble."

"Shit Ralph!" Meg began her tirade, "You'll be in trouble…big trouble if the Department finds out. The fact that she just turned nineteen and you're sixty-five should have said something to you. If nothing else, for crying out loud, you're old enough to be her fucking Grandfather!"

"I know I've acted improperly. I know that if this gets out, it will bring embarrassment to the Department. And, shame to an otherwise impeccable career," countered Doyle. "But my concern now is Amanda and her safety."

"Meg asked, "Well can you tell me about your investigation? I mean I don't even know if I can be of any help. Who knows, maybe someone outside of the scope of things could pick up on something you have overlooked. Maybe you're too close. Does that make sense?"

Doyle began to give her an education, both about his investigation and the White Supremacist Group he had been monitoring. "They call themselves the 'Guardians of Israel' and they are truly hardcore Nazi's!" Nazi's and Israel used in the same descriptor totally confused Meg and she questioned Doyle. "What the hell are you saying? Nazi's and Jews were ardent enemies?"

Doyle knew this was going to take some time and explained to Meg that he completely understood her confusion, but, at the same time, told her to be patient and just follow along. Doyle was confident that he could clarify things for Meg. "You see Meg, although these skinheads are Nazi's, they believe that Adolf Hitler and the Third Reich knew what was best for the Aryan Race."

Doyle explained that the skinheads took the teaching of Hitler and combined them with selected teachings of Christian identity. Doyle told Meg that the group adhered to Adamic Race, or Adamic Bloodline. Doyle asked, "Are you still with me?" "So far, so good," Meg responded. "I don't really understand what Adamic is or how it relates to Nazi's or Israel for that matter."

Doyle nodded and continued. "Okay, I'll run this down for you step by step." Doyle opened yet another beer and began to put forth his best effort to teach Meg all he could about his work. "Skinheads are Neo-Nazi Racists full of hate for all non-whites, Jews and homosexuals. Any white man or woman who dates or marries outside of their race is in fact a 'Race Trader' and an instant enemy of the Aryan peoples. Now introduce these kids who are full of hate to the Christian Identity. Identity teaches that Adam and Eve were made in the image of God. Both Adam and Eve were white and therefore God is white."

Doyle explained, "It's referred to as the 'Two Seed Ideology', wherein Adam and Eve in a union produced Abel. Eve was tempted by a serpent to eat an apple from the Tree of Knowledge. There was an act by Satan to seduce Eve. Cain was produced from this union. Cain and Abel were twins with different fathers. Because he was not racially pure, Cain could not participate in God's Grand Plan for the white race and killed Abel out of jealousy. Cain was banned from Eden, and according to the 'Two Seed Ideology', Cain became the father of the Jewish Race, making Jews the Children of Satan."

Doyle paused and took a manly swig of his beer and asked Meg if she was able to follow along thus far. Meg responded, "Wow, these guys are really out there, aren't they? But I get it so far. Keep going, I'll stop you if I have any questions."

"Okay then," Doyle said as he continued. "Adam and Eve produced a third son, Seth. Seth was born to replace Abel and continue the Adamic bloodline. An Adamite who maintained his racial purity was Noah. Noah himself produced three sons. However, it was Noah's son, Shem, who maintained his own racial purity by marrying a white woman. Shem's followers became known as the Shemites (Semites.) Identity claims they cannot be Anti-Semitic, as they are the true Semites."

"The next important biblical figure to Christian Identity is Abraham. God made a covenant with Abraham, who fathered Isaac, to whom he passed the covenant. Isaac had two sons, Jacob and Esau, which has been interpreted as Isaac's sons or Saxons. Esau married a Canaanite woman violating God's covenant. Jacob was given the name Israel (Ish-Ra-Eli), which translates, 'He will rule with God'. Christian Identity interprets this to mean that the white race is the true Biblical Israelites and not the Jews, as commonly taught."

"Jacob produced twelve sons. Each of whom had families so large that they became known as Tribes. The Tribes took the name of the founding son. For example: The Tribe of Levi became the Levites. The Tribe of Joseph was divided by his two sons Ephram and Manasseh, each of whom received the name of Israel."

Doyle again took a sip of beer as he uttered, "now, if I have done the math correctly this completes the thirteen tribes which we had been told were lost. Christian Identity, however, teaches that the Tribes of Israel were not lost. The Tribes were actually captured and taken to an area near the Southern region of the Caspian Sea. After assimilating with local populations, the descendants of the Nation of Israel began a twelve-century-long migration to the northwest. This trek took them across the Caucasus Mountains."

Doyle chuckled as he drank the final drops from the long neck. "Can you believe that we became known as Caucasians because of the mountain range? Now here is where the Guardians of Israel begins to make sense. You see, the Tribe of Ephraim settled in Great Britain. Ephraim, as you recall had been given the name 'Israel.' This had led to the concept known as 'British Israelism.'"

"Now, Ephraim's brother, Manassah, had also been given the name of Israel. The descendants of Manasseh came to America on the Mayflower and settled in the New World. These settlers brought with them 'The Eagle,' the Great Seal of Manasseh. Christian Identity contends that the United States is the true Israel. Not only is the Eagle the Great Seal of the Tribe of Manasseh, it is the Seal of the United States. But their belief also contends that God said that Old Jerusalem would be destroyed, and a New Jerusalem given them. The New Jerusalem would have great seas to the east and west, with great mountains and rivers in between. God vowed that this New Jerusalem would never be defeated in war."

"So, you can see, the skinheads call themselves 'The Guardians of Israel' because they believe that the United States is the true Israel. And, that the Adamites, or Adamic bloodline is the true descendants of Israel."

Doyle was now talked out and out of beer. Doyle also realized that he had not visited the bathroom since his arrival. Doyle excused himself. Sully watched as his friend entered the house and headed toward Meg, who actually met him in the middle of the yard. Sully asked, "What's up with Ralph? Everything Okay with him?"

Meg began with, "He is conflicted over the disappearance of an informant. And, I would have to say that not everything is Okay with him." Sully suggested they ask Ralph to stay the night. Meg agreed. Not only was Doyle upset and obviously depressed, he was intoxicated and in no condition to drive. Just then Doyle walked out of the house with a fresh beer in his hand. Doyle joined his dear friends in the middle of the yard.

Doyle asked, "Well Sully," his words slightly slurred, "how have you been?" Sully, reaching out and putting his right hand on Doyle's left shoulder stated, "It's been a very busy year for me old buddy. Meg tells me you have been feeling some job-related pressure of late. To tell you the truth Ralph, you look like you're worn out. Why don't you stay the night with us? We'll start you out tomorrow with a good home-cooked breakfast. How about it?"

"No. Thanks, but, no. I need to go home and review some paperwork," Doyle replied. Sully quipped, "Come on Ralph. You'll go home and just pass out. You know you've had a lot to drink. You should not be behind the wheel of a car and you know it!"

Doyle agreed, "I'll tell you what. I'll let you take me home. I'll get my car later in the week. Does that sound fair to you?" Sully nodded in agreement knowing full well this was the best he was going to get out of Doyle. However, Meg spoke up, "I'll drive you home. You're not the only one who's been socking them away. Sully, you have been drinking all day. You're not going to be doing any driving either."

CHAPTER III

THE GUARDIANS OF ISRAEL

O N THE DRIVE TO DOYLE'S RESIDENCE, RALPH leaning back in the passenger seat realized that he had neglected to tell Meg about the Guardians of Israel themselves. He had given her a Sunday School lesson on what their beliefs are and why. Doyle reached down and turned the radio off and at the same time looked at Meg. "There's more," he said. Meg could detect hesitance in Doyle's voice. She knew that Doyle wanted to unload on her everything he knew about the Skinheads. But yet, at the same time, he was afraid to involve her. Meg opened the door. "So, tell me. I know you analyzed your thoughts and you have come to your own conclusions. So just tell me everything and we'll see where it all leads us."

Doyle began with, "Justin Davis was a twenty-one-year-old hard-core Neo-Nazi. Justin was all tatted with White Power signs, including the word 'Israel' tattooed in the Rune Alphabet, with a swastika on either side. This tattoo, which Doyle Drew on a notepad, was on the back of Justin's neck." Doyle told Meg that Justin had been Amanda's boyfriend and that Justin had pulled Amanda into the Movement. Justin, according to Doyle, was the Group's Leader.

Meg interrupted, "Doyle, just how many of these guys are there anyway?" Doyle admitted that he did not know exactly just how many members the Guardians of Israel had. However, he had up to this point, identified 23 young men and 16 young women. Doyle told Meg that Amanda had reported to him that one of the girls, sixteen-year-old Robin Peterson, gave her the impression that she was not comfortable with the Group. Amanda had suggested that Doyle should contact Robin and attempt to turn her.

The one thing that Doyle wanted to impress upon Meg was that the Guardians were extremely violent. Ralph told Meg that there was no doubt in his mind that the Skinheads would do everything they could to eliminate their perceived enemies. Ralph clarified further that the Skinheads were capable of inciting a race war.

Doyle felt that the Guardians were actively involved in criminal activity, but he had not yet connected them to any definite criminal acts. As Meg reached Doyle's house, Doyle turned and said, "Meg, I know that these race freaks did something to Amanda. I am sick over this. I know I pushed her too hard. I asked too much of her. They found her out. I am sure of it. The last time I heard from her was three days ago. She told me that she had reason to believe that the Guardians had been involved in some homosexual murders. She told me she would get more specific details and call me."

Doyle was almost in tears. Meg was surprised by this display of emotion by this old tough guy Detective. Meg again asked. "Ralph, why don't you just come back home with me? Sully and I would love to have you spend a few days with us. Then we can talk about this some more." Doyle smiled, squeezed Meg's hand and said, "Thanks Meg. I'll be fine. With a good night's sleep, I'll get my head clear and get back to the job at hand." Doyle got out of the car and walked onto the porch. He opened the door and as he entered the house, he turned and waved goodbye to Meg.

As Meg arrived back at home, her sister and brother-in-law, Lara and Robert, were just getting ready to go home. During their exchange of hugs and handshakes, Robert asked about Doyle. Meg explained that he was very troubled and with good reason. Meg related, "You know, I can't explain it in the true sense of things, but Ralph is an emotional wreck. He is like a broken man."

Sully knew Meg very well. He knew she was not one to over exaggerate, nor downplay anything. Sully assured them, "I'll meet

THE GUARDIANS OF ISRAEL

him for lunch tomorrow and see what I can do to help him out."
With that said, everyone agreed to call it a night. After Robert and
Lara left, Meg took a quick look around to see where she should
start with the clean up. To her surprise, everything had been
picked up and put away. She looked at Sully and question, "What
did I miss?" Sully laughed, "Well, how you pretty much missed
everything after the cake. Ralph had you cornered in the yard and
the two of you were so wrapped up in your little talk that you were
oblivious to the goings on around you."

"I'm sorry," Meg confessed. Sully added, "No, no, Meg. I'm
trying to put a guilt trip on you. It's fine. Doyle needed an ear and I
am glad you were there for him." Meg gave Sully a kiss and led him
into the house. They were both exhausted and looked forward to a
goodnight's sleep.

Monday morning seemed to roll around a little sooner than
anyone really desired. Sully turned off the alarm, walked down the
hall and looked in on Shawn. As he re-entered the master bedroom,
he patted Meg's butt, which was protected under the covers. Sully
told Meg that the one- year-old was still sound asleep. He suggested
that Meg stay in bed as long as she could.

He would stop at Starbucks for a cup of house blend coffee and
perhaps a raspberry scone on his way into the station.

It was 7:30 a.m. when Sully pulled into Newton Street Station.
After settling in at his desk with a fresh cup of coffee, he began
going through a stack of reports on his desk. Sully was relieved to
see that the reports were follow-up reports that he had done earlier
on other cases. They had all been approved and the work copies
were returned to him. He was happy to see that no new cases had
been assigned to him while he was in Eureka. By the time Sully
put the reports in their appropriate case books, Mary walked in
from Records. She had a six-page fax in hand. It was from Mark
Campbell from the District Attorney's Office in Eureka. Sully
smiled at Mary and thanked her for bringing him what would prove
to be a strong closing argument in the final trial of the Masey Gang.

Before he knew it, time had slipped by. It was just after 12 noon
and Sully had meant to call Ralph Doyle for lunch. What Sully
didn't know though was that Doyle failed to show up to work today.

It was also uncharacteristic of Doyle not to even call in. Sully also had no way of knowing that Doyle's co-workers had tried numerous times to reach him on both his cell and home phones.

It was pushing 12:30 p.m. when Lieutenant Hampton walked up to Sully's desk. "Detective Sullivan," he said as he cleared his throat. "Captain Morton from Major Crimes Division just called." Major Crimes Division was relatively new to the Department. It was a major part of the Homeland Security Bureau. "M.C.D" as it was called, was comprised of the Anti-Terrorist Division (both the Intelligence and the Criminal Investigation Sections), the Criminal Conspiracy Section and the Special Investigation Section.

Lieutenant Hampton continued, "The Captain wants you out at Ralph Doyle's house." Sully smiled, "I knew he would be too hung over to make it into work." Lt. Hampton again cleared his throat, "Sully. Doyle has been murdered. I'm sorry. I know the two of you were close." "Murdered!" Sully uttered as he shook his head. "No! This can't be! How does a tough cop like Doyle get murdered? Not in his own house! No! Maybe on the street... maybe when some punk gets off a luck shot in a dark alley... but. No! Not in his own home!"

Lt. Hampton decided to send another Detective with Sully. Hampton thought Sully was too upset by the news and assigned the task of driving to Detective Jim Anderson. As Sully and Anderson pulled in front of Doyle's house, they were met by Captain Morton. The house itself was in the Highland Park Area of Los Angeles. Doyle had only recently purchased the home from his Uncle. The home was built in the thirties at a time when pride in workmanship was evident in the home's intricate woodwork.

Captain Morton pulled Sully aside and away from Anderson and the others. It was apparent to Sully that this was going to be a private conversation. Morton began by telling Sully that Doyle was executed by White Supremacists. It was most likely a group Doyle was investigating. Morton added that Sully would understand how the Captain reached this conclusion once he, himself observed the crime scene.

Morton then gave Sully the good news that would add to his discomfort "By the way Detective, you should know that the

THE GUARDIANS OF ISRAEL

Homicide Boys at Northeast Division are.... shall we keep it clean.... and.... shall we say, just say a bit put off by you being brought into this case." Sully knew just how the Detectives might feel about being cut out of a homicide that, rightfully so, should be theirs to investigate. After all, Sully himself would be upset if the shoe were on the other foot. On the other hand, Sully also knew that a case involving the murder of a fellow police officer would be taken over by the Robbery Homicide Division at Parker Center.

Sully acknowledged Morton. "Cappy. I can deal with the guys from Northeast. But, what about the boys from downtown? You know that they are going to want to take this over." Morton was thinking to himself, nobody besides Doyle had ever called him "Cappy." Which is in itself, an old friendly tag given to Captains on the Department. Although a dying term, it is still used at times by "Old Salts". Morton looked at Sully and said with authority, "The Chief stands behind me on this one. He also thinks that you're the best guy to have head up this investigation."

Sully, along with Captain Morton, walked up the steps to the front porch. The porch spanned the width of the front of the house. Constructed of wood planks, it was painted forest green to match the trim of the otherwise white wood siding of the home. Captain Morton introduced Sully to Detective III Richard Andrews, the Homicide Coordinator at Northeast Division. Sullivan, himself a Detective II, was extremely cognizant of both rank and time on the job. Sully was respectful of Andrew's stature. Not only was he a Detective III grade, he was a Homicide Coordinator and that meant a great deal to Sully. Sully did feel that he himself merited the same respect. After all, he had nearly five years in seniority on Andrews. And, after all, Sully worked Newton Street Homicide, one of the busiest homicide units in the City.

Sully reached his hand out and stated, "Detective Andrews, sir. I know that I am intruding into your space here and I apologize. But the Department did bring me into this case." "You know Detective," Andrews replied as he took Sully's hand and smiled, "it's all part of twenty." Sully grinned. He knew that egos were not going to get in the way. All part of twenty was a cop's way of saying "shit happens", and after twenty years, it wouldn't matter. Twenty years

23

was the amount of time a cop would have to put in until his, or her pension would be vested. Sully nodded and simply stated, "Thanks."

Andrews continued, "I understand Detective Doyle was a close friend. And, I also know that being too close to an investigation could cloud one's judgment. So... I want to offer my assistance for nothing more than a 'what if.' This meaning, when you get to a point in your investigation where if, in the continuation in your course you might damage your friend's reputation. But, on the hand, if you sway from your direction you may compromise the integrity of your investigation…. That's the 'what if' I'll be there to help you with."

Andrews smiled and gave a single nod. Sully returned the smile. And, with a nod, he responded with a simple, "Deal." Sully entered Doyle's home. The front door led directly into the living room. The room measured 15-feet wide by 20-feet in length. Adjoining the living room was a formal dining room, 13-feet wide and 16-feet in length. The dining room had a built-in china cabinet against the far wall. The living room and dining room were separated by two wooden floor and ceiling pillars. The pillars were spaced 6 feet apart creating the entry into the dining room. The space between the pillars and walls was filled in by built in cabinets standing 3-feet in height and matching the design of the china cabinet. This type of construction was very common in Los Angeles in the 1930's and early 40's.

Sully stood in the doorway for a moment in horror at what he was seeing. His good friend's body was hung suspended between the pillars. Doyle's body hung there nude. His hands and feet were tied with leather straps and the straps were nailed to the wooden pillars. Sully could only describe the visual appearance of the way Doyle hung there by comparing it to the old Cingular logo.

Written in blood on the living room wall was "Race Traitor." Sully examined his friend's body and found two wounds. First, was Doyle's right index finger. It had been amputated. Sully surmised that Doyle's attackers had cut off his finger and used it as a pencil to write the words "Race Traitor" on the wall. The second wound was a four inch by four-inch Star of David branded into the flesh of Doyle's chest. There was no way to determine the cause of death as yet, but it did appear that Doyle was still alive when he was branded.

As for other physical evidence at the crime scene, it was slim pickens. There was no evidence of forced entry, therefore leading Sully to believe that the suspects may have been laying in wait. The boys from the lab had not been able to obtain latent prints. Nor had anyone been able to locate Doyle's severed finger.

The investigative process at the crime scene was slow and methodical. The lab boys spent hours searching for forensics and it was late into the night when things wrapped up at Doyle's home. As Sully stepped out onto the front porch, he noticed the cars parked on the street and noted that almost every car on the street belonged to the LAPD. Sully felt that a car parked on the street the previous night, especially one not belonging in the neighborhood, would surely have been noticed by neighbors.

Sully then had an eerie feeling. The feeling had been delayed as a result of Sully's full attention being directed at the crime scene investigation. But none the less, the feeling was now present. It had occurred to Sully that Meg had driven Doyle home the previous night. Had the suspects been laying in wait, and had Meg gone in the house to ensure Doyle would be Okay if left alone, then she too could have been a victim as well.

When Sully's concern turned to relief, he realized that Meg maybe able to shed some light on things. After all, she did spend most of the previous evening talking to Doyle. Doyle himself may have divulged things to Meg that could possibly give some direction to the investigation at hand. As Sully walked out into the street to where Anderson was waiting with the car, Sully thought again about the lack of civilian cars parked on the street in Doyle's neighborhood. Sully knew that the first witness he would be interviewing was his own wife, Meg. Did she happen to see the murderers' vehicle?

CHAPTER IV

WITNESS WITH A KISS

I T WAS LATE THAT NIGHT WHEN SULLY GOT HOME. IN fact, Meg was in bed and the tonight show with Jay Leno had just begun. Sully sat down on the edge of Meg's side of the bed. He turned on the lamp which was on Meg's nightstand. Meg looked up at Sully. She could read the sorrow in his eyes. "Oh Shit, Sully!" She questioned, with a quivering voice, "What is it?" Sully responded, "Meg...... Doyle was murdered at his home sometime last night." Meg grabbed Sully in a bear hug of an embrace. Meg now in tears gave Sully a long hard kiss. A kiss that showed love, as well as fear for the safety of the cop she loved. Sully explained what had happened at Doyle's home. He described the ritualistic fashion in which the homicide took place. He told her about the words on the wall that were written in Doyle's own blood. Sully went on to explain that Captain Morton felt that Doyle was killed by a White Supremacist Group that Doyle might have been looking at.

Sully then looked at his wife and gave her the news. "You're my best witness to date. I believe that Doyle, in his conversation with you last night, divulged information that could be very important to his murder investigation. I can only tell you that I am relieved that you didn't go into his house with him. Or you too could have been killed. The other thing that I need to ask you is, and you really need to think about this question. Did you see any suspicious cars parked on the street near Ralph's home?"

Meg was in shock. Yet, she was still able to keep her senses about her. Meg could not fathom the reality that Doyle had been murdered. He was one of those "Old Salt" Detectives that you went to for an answer to any problem. He was a tough old guy who didn't take shit off of anyone. Doyle had massive hands and when he reached out and gangster slapped you…well, he surely had your full attention. Meg thought for a minute and responded to Sully's question. "No, I can't remember seeing a single car on the street. But you know I was just watching Ralph walk up to his front porch. He had stopped before going up the steps. He turned to wave goodbye. And, at the same time he showed me that he had his keys. So, I drove off. I didn't see anyone else on the street."

Sully asked Meg if it would have been possible for suspects to hide in the bushes near the front porch. Or even on the porch without being detected by her. Meg acknowledged that someone could have hidden in the area of the front porch without being detected from the street. Meg then related to Sully what Doyle had told her the night before. She told him about how Doyle had told her about his sexual relations with the 19-year old Skinhead informant, Amanda Cavanaugh. Meg told Sully about the Guardians of Israel, the Neo-Nazi Skinheads that Doyle had been investigating. Meg told Sully that Doyle had explained it all to her, but that she would need time to collect her thoughts before she could explain it to him. The fact of the matter was that she was exhausted and her mind would not stay focused. Her thoughts kept returning to Ralph Doyle and the inconceivable thought that he had been murdered.

Sully thought that perhaps, after a good night's sleep, if at all possible, they would have a more productive exchange of information. Sully told Meg that they would call Meg's sister, Clara, in the morning and see if she could watch Shawn. Then the two of them could go into work and go over what Doyle had told Meg.

It was about 8:00 o'clock in the morning when Sully and Meg rolled out of bed. Sully took the first shower, while Meg got Shawn up and ready for a day with his Aunt Clara and Uncle Robert. After Sully was dressed, Meg jumped in for a quick splash in the hot shower. Sully prepared breakfast for the two of them and at the same time fed Shawn Patrick.

After dropping Shawn off at Clara and Robert's, Sully drove Meg to Newton Street Division. Sully knew that he would have to actually interview Meg at Major Crimes Division along with Captain Morton, but first Sully needed to meet and confer with Lt. Hampton. Hampton was the Lieutenant in Charge of Newton Detectives. Since the Homicide Coordinator was on vacation, Lieutenant Hampton was his next immediate supervisor. After briefing the Lieutenant on the murder of Detective Doyle, Sully inserted his own thoughts on the case. He included his wife's role, not only as a witness, but as an advisor. After the briefing, Sully completed his overtime report for the previous workday. He gathered Meg and the two drove to the Offices of Major Crimes Division.

Sully and Meg checked in with the receptionist at M.C.D. They were given Visitor passes and escorted to Captain Morton's Office. Morton greeted them at his door and invited them into his office. As the three sat down at the table, Sully explained to the Captain that his wife had driven Doyle home the night he was murdered. Sully explained that Doyle had been at their home Sunday celebrating their son's first birthday. Sully told Morton that Doyle had been drinking and because he was intoxicated and depressed over the disappearance of an informant, he had poured his soul out to Meg. Captain Morton interrupted and asked Meg, "What did Doyle tell you?" Meg looked at Sully for guidance. She knew that if she divulged the relationship between Doyle and his informant Amanda Cavanaugh, Doyle's reputation and good name would be smeared. Meg thought she could hide this information, at least for awhile. Sully saw the indecision in Meg's face and instructed, "Meg, tell him everything. Don't spare him any of the details no matter how harmful you think they might be to Doyle."

Meg began by telling Morton that Doyle was out of sorts Sunday evening. That he had been extremely concerned about a young female informant that had failed to report in. Doyle hadn't heard from the girl for three days, Meg related. Meg told Sully and Captain Morton that Doyle's informant believed that the Skinheads, known as The Guardians of Israel, were involved in some recent homosexual murders. Captain Morton again jumped in with a question for Meg. "Did Ralph tell you who his informant was?" Meg answered, "Yes sir he did. Her name is Amanda Cavanaugh. Amanda had told Doyle that she was close to learning the specifics relative to these murders."

Meg paused, "Ah.... There's one more thing you should know about Doyle and this informant." Captain Morton raised an eyebrow with interest and asked, "This is not going to be good, is it?" Meg continued, "Doyle and the girl were involved." Meg wouldn't say they were sexually involved. She just couldn't bring herself to completely discredit Doyle. But then she didn't have to. Captain Morton knew exactly what she meant.

"Okay," Morton said. "We will deal with that later. Let's continue with what Doyle had to tell you about the Skinheads." Meg searched her memory for the details given to her by Doyle. She related that Doyle had identified several members of the Guardians of Israel including twenty-three young men and sixteen young girls. Meg reported that Doyle had told her that a twenty-one-year-old, known as Justin Davis, was the Group's Leader. She also related that Doyle had told her that a sixteen-year-old Skinhead girl, named Robin Peterson, was approachable and may be turned.

Captain Morton nodded with gratitude and told both Sully and Meg that he would have one of his Intelligence Detectives go through Doyle's desk and review his files on the Guardians. Morton told Sully that he wanted him to conduct most of his work out of M.C.D. office space. Morton then asked Meg if she would put in her Reserve Officer work hours assisting her husband. To which, of course, she agreed. Morton advised that he would work on getting Visitor passes, to come and go, to the M.C.D. office space at will.

Sully agreed to do the bulk of his work on the murder case of Ralph Doyle within earshot of the Captain. Sully advised that if Morton was satisfied up to this point, he would like to return to Newton Street to work on a teletype and contact the Los Angeles Coroner's Office. Morton gave Sully free rein. He said, "Sully, you know what needs to be done. I am not going to get in your way. I just want to be kept up to snuff on this. I don't expect you to be in my line of sight at all times. But the fact is, that Doyle has files here. These are files that cannot leave the office. However, I am confident that you, with the help of your wife Meg, will find leads that will help you nab the bastards that did this to Doyle."

Upon returning to Newton Street, Sully telephoned the Los Angeles Coroner's Office. Sully's call was directed to the Senior Examiner, Bill Casey. Sully, of course, wanted to learn the cause of death. Casey was able to tell Sully that they had found a small puncture to a vein in Doyle's arm. Casey said the puncture was consistent with that of a hypodermic needle. Sully asked, "Do you think he was given a hot shot?" A hot shot is a term used to describe an intentional drug overdose. Casey replied, "Sorry old buddy, too early to tell. We are running toxicology and testing some tissue samples. It may take a couple of days. Now, before you jump all over me, let me assure you that this is top priority in our office. I'll let you know when we know. Good enough?" Sully knew that Bill Casey and his team would work through the night if need-be to identify the cause of death. Sully let Casey know that he understood and would be patient.

Sully began to put together a statewide teletype alerting law enforcement agencies as to the murder of a Los Angeles Police Detective. In the teletype Sully would enter certain details, such as the strange position the nude body was found suspended in air, as it were. Sully would note the severed finger and the fact that it had not been recovered at the crime scene. Sully would include the fact that the victim had been ritualistically branded but would not describe the mark left on the body. Sully would note that the words "Race Traitor" had been written in the victim's blood on the wall near the body. Sully delivered the draft of his teletype to the Records Unit so that it could be sent out. Afterwards, Sully and Meg met with Lieutenant Hampton and briefed him on the meeting that they had with Captain Morton.

The day was winding down, but Sully felt antsy and thought a trip to the morgue was in order. Sully grabbed Meg and drove to Los Angeles County General Hospital. The Coroner's Office was located at the hospital and Sully wanted a face-to-face with Bill Casey. For the most part the Coroner's Office was vacant. The lights were on, but it didn't look like anyone but the stiffs were home. Sully yelled out, "Hey, anyone around?" His voice echoed back and forth between the empty halls. "Quiet you idiot! Do you want to wake the dead?" It was a familiar voice. That of Bill Casey. Sully followed the sound and found Casey working on Ralph Doyle's cadaver. Sully, leading Meg into the room by her hand, introduced her to Casey and they exchanged the usual pleasantries.

Casey immediately began to explain his examination of Doyle's body. Casey pointed to the injection mark on Doyle's right arm. Casey told Sully that Doyle died of a poison that was injected directly into his bloodstream. Sully, of course, asked Bill, "What poison?" Casey hesitated, "Well, I'm not a hundred percent sure but it looks like it's going to be Ricin." Meg interjected, "Ricin? What is Ricin?" Casey answered, "It's a poison derived from the castor bean. It's known as the 'Assassin's Poison'." Sully added, "Ricin is a poison highly touted by White Supremacist Groups." Sully asked Bill Casey when he could say for sure. Casey rocked his head back and forth hemming and hawing and then just came out with it. "Look Sully, it's Ricin! I would take that to the bank! Okay? It's just that for the Judicial System, if you will, we have to go through a few more steps. But, if it helps you to know now, then go with Ricin because I don't believe that we are going to find anything else."

CHAPTER V

BAKERSFIELD

I T WAS WEDNESDAY MORNING AND SULLY HAD JUST SAT down at his desk when the phone rang. Sully answered, "Detective Sullivan, Newton Homicide. May I help you?" As it turned out, Sully's teletype paid off. It was Lieutenant Gene Johnson, the Day Watch Watch Commander of the Bakersfield Police Department. "Yes Sir, this is Lieutenant Johnson, Bakersfield Police Department. I have your teletype regarding the murder of a Police Detective. We have just found the body of a female murder victim up here that fits your modus operandi. Our Homicide people want to know if you can make a trip up here and examine the crime scene yourself before they remove the body?" Sully, without hesitating stated, "I'll be there as soon as I can. Can you give me a location and a contact number for someone at the scene?" After getting the address of the crime location and directions, as well as, a cell phone number for Detective Richard Hughes, Sully called Captain Morton. Sully told Morton of the Bakersfield case and the possibility that the victim could be Doyle's missing informant. Morton interjected, "I'll have a helicopter standing by at Parker Center to take us to Bakersfield."

Sully didn't question Captain Morton. He knew that Morton had a lot of influence and for him to get a helicopter at the drop of a hat did not surprise him. What did surprise Sully was the fact that Morton was making the trip with him. Sully called Detective Hughes to let him know that he, along with Captain Morton would be flying up in a police helicopter. Hughes gave Sully the location of a closed warehouse, a half block away from the crime scene.

Sully met Captain Morton on the roof of Parker Center; just as Air Three was approaching the helipad. Officer Townsend, the observer, assisted Sully and Captain Morton with seatbelts and headsets. The pilot, Officer Jackson, welcomed the two aboard and the flight began. From lift off at Parker Center in downtown Los Angeles to landing in Bakersfield took just about forty-five minutes. Detective Hughes was waiting in the empty parking lot of the warehouse when Air Three touched down.

Detective Hughes, Captain Morton and Detective Sullivan completed a round of self introductions. "We want to thank you," Sully stated, "for bringing us in on this so early. Your Lieutenant Johnson told me that you had just discovered the body this morning." "Yes," Hughes responded, "we got the call at about 7:30 this morning. The house has been vacant for about three months. It's still a probate property, but the family members that are going to inherit the house wanted to get a jump on fixing it up. The painter opened the front door and discovered the body. Actually, they told me that they noted a very strong and very foul odor when they first walked up onto the porch. Our patrol officers arrived and secured the scene. When I got here and took a look inside, I saw the girl hanging there suspended by all four limbs, and the words 'Race Traitor' written on the wall. Well, your teletype read exactly what I was now seeing."

Sully thanked Hughes as the three of them entered the unmarked Detective Unit to drive to the crime scene. Affixed to the front of the house on Maple Street was the address: 1512. It was a tan, stucco, single family house with a brown composition shingle roof. The wood trim was painted white. The stucco paint, as well as, the trim was peeling and flaking off its surface. The lawn was dead as was most of the shrubbery. The house had most likely been built in the early 1950's.

Hughes led Captain Morton and Sully up to the front porch. The smell was horrid. Sully had been told by Meg that Doyle told her Sunday at Shawn's birthday party that his informant had not been heard from for three days. Sully concluded that if this victim was Amanda Cavanaugh, that she could have been dead for as much as six days. Sully stood at the front porch and lit up one of his cigars. He then offered one to Captain Morton and Detective Hughes. "Cappy," he said, "you might want to smoke one of these. It will help to mask the smell of death." Hughes interjected, "does that really work? I have heard some of the old timers say that it does, but I've never actually had one of these smellers before."

Sully assured the two that the cigar smell really did help to tolerate the smell of a decomposed body. With three cigars now filling the room with a more tolerable aroma, the trio entered the living room. Sully noted the words "Race Traitor" written on the wall in what appeared to be dried blood. The naked female body, with leather straps tied to her four limbs, were stretched out and nailed to the wood jams that created the five-foot passage into the dining room. Sully noted that the girl's right index finger had been amputated in the same manner as his friend, Ralph Doyle. The girl had also been branded on her chest, centered above her breasts. It too was a four inch by four-inch Star of David.

The body itself was too decomposed to detect bruising. However, there were two distinctive burn marks on the body, one at the back of the neck, and the other at the top of the pubic line. "Enough," Sully yelled out to Captain Morton and Detective Hughes. "Let's go out into some fresh air!"

After reaching the sidewalk Captain Morton asked, "Well Sully, what's your take?" Sully told the two that it was obviously the same suspects that killed Detective Doyle in Los Angles. Sully directed his thoughts to Detective Hughes. "How long have your lab boys been at it there in the house?" Hughes replied, "They got here about an hour ago, so they still have their work cut out for them."

Sully thought that it would be the better part of the day until the scientific investigative unit of the Bakersfield Police Department would be done with their examination of the crime scene. Sully could see the Kern County Coroner's van parked on the street and figured it was just a matter of time before the body was removed. Sully looked at Captain Morton. "Hey Cap, why don't we head

back to Los Angeles and let these guys do their job?" Sully then
included Detective Hughes, Howard Hughes, and no relationship to
the creator of the Spruce Goose. He was young and relatively new
to the Detective Bureau of the Bakersfield Police Department. The
fact was that Hughes had never handled a homicide investigation
before.

"Howard," Sully began, "how about we get out of your hair for
now? It's clear that your homicide here is directly related to ours.
Your victim is obviously our missing informant. So, my thought is,
I'll go back to L.A. and then meet you tomorrow, say 2:00? I'll bring
a fingerprint packet that I believe will match your girl here. That
will give you a positive identification. You and I can go over what, if
anything, your lab boys come up with. Then, we'll go over and see
what the Coroner can give us."

Hughes agreed and said he would let the Coroner know that
they would meet him at 3:00. Sully concurred and then added,
"Howard. One more thought. Why not tell the Coroner that
the victim may very well have been tortured to obtain certain
information?" Hughes nodded and assured Sully that he would pass
that information on to the Coroner. Hughes then drove Captain
Morton and Sully back to the awaiting helicopter. On the flight
back to Los Angeles, Officer Townsend asked his passengers if they
had any luck with the investigation. A question they answered in the
affirmative. Sully and Captain Morton did not discuss the details of
the case the entire ride back.

Most of the investigation was confidential and the areas that
were not confidential were, at the very least, sensitive. Anything that
was said into the headset would be heard by everyone wearing one.
After landing on the roof of Parker Center, Captain Morton and
Sully walked down the staircase. Captain Morton stated, "Sully,
I told you before that I wasn't going to hound you. And, I know
that in reality I am hounding you. It's just that this is personal to
me. Doyle was more than an Intelligence Detective that worked
under me. Doyle was an icon at the Anti-Terrorist Section of Major
Crimes. There was nothing about the ins and outs of Intel that he
did not know. Sully, I can't count the number of times I went to
Doyle for advice. I want these bastards! And, if I am a pest about

it, then I'm sorry." Sully nodded, "I understand Cap. I don't mind. This means a lot to me as well."

After briefing Lieutenant Hampton at Newton Street, Sully checked out a black and white unit. Sully knew his workday would be consumed by his visit to Bakersfield tomorrow afternoon. Bakersfield was a good hour and a half drive from Los Angeles. Sully did not want to be delayed by being stopped by the California Highway Patrol for speed. The best pace car on the interstate is a black and white. And, so a black and white would be Sully's mode of transportation for the day.

When Sully got home, he told Meg of the Bakersfield girl. Sully explained that the girl's body was too decomposed to identify. Meg stated, "Well, Doyle told me she had white power tattoos. Did you see Nazi SS lightening bolts on the back of her neck or a swastika just below her bikini line?" Sully said, "Oh shit! That's why!" Meg questioned, "What's why?" Sully explained, "The girl in Bakersfield was branded with the Star of David exactly like Doyle. But then there were two burn marks on her body. One was on the back of her neck and the other just at the top of her pussy hair.

It was easy for both Sully and Meg to conclude from this that the victim was Doyle's informant. The Skinheads killed her in the same fashion. They dubbed her a "Race Traitor" and stripped her of any marking of White Supremacy. Sully thought it's like her tattoos were badges of merit that she had to earn in the Movement. And, now they had been stripped away. Sully related this thought to Meg who responded, "You're probably right about that Sully. You know they must have beaten her mercilessly to get her to tell them about Doyle. I mean it's no doubt that they would have beaten her anyway for betraying them. That poor girl. Nobody should die like that. No one should die in the manner that Ralph did either. But, at least, they didn't beat and torture him."

It was 1:45 Thursday afternoon when Sully arrived at the Bakersfield Police Department. Detective Hughes served up a cup of coffee for his guest as the two sat down to talk about the physical evidence found in the Maple Street house. As it turned out, the crime scene was as clean of forensics as was Doyle's home. The only key piece of evidence was that of the missing index finger. Sully surmised that one of the Skinhead suspects was collecting trophies. It was Sully's conclusion that when he had identified his suspect, he would recover the finger of his friend Doyle, along with the finger of Amanda Cavanaugh.

Sully, although disappointed in the absence of crime scene evidence, was not surprised. Sully then told Hughes that he believed the burn marks left on the girl's nape, and pubic line were placed there to burn off the white power tattoos that she had.

The two detectives arrived at the Coroner's office and met with Dr. Chad Hastings, the Medical Examiner. Sully handed Hastings a copy of Amanda Cavanaugh's fingerprints stating, "I know the body was pretty nasty. But hopefully you were able to retrieve enough prints for identification." Hastings informed Hughes and Sully that he did manage to get some lifts from the body. Enough to make an I.D. anyway. The doctor led the Detectives into the examination room where Amanda's nude body laid on the table. Dr. Hastings began explaining the girl's injuries, "The examination shows a broken jaw and a broken cheekbone on the left side of her face. She suffered two skull fractures, and each of her left-hand fingers had been broken, possibly with a pair of pliers." Hastings added, "And, of course, you already noted that her right index finger had been amputated."

Sully then questioned, "Doc, did you notice any needle marks? You see in our homicide in Los Angeles the cause of death was due to an injection of Ricin." Hastings told Sully that he had not found any injection marks. But he assured both Detectives that they would test the body for poisons and other substances. Dr. Hastings added that he would get right on the fingerprints as well in order to positively identify Amanda Cavanaugh.

On the way back to Detective Hughes' office, Sully explained that he had some good leads in the case. Sully informed Hughes that he was confident that the girl was killed by members of a Neo-Nazi Skinhead group known as the Guardians of Israel. Sully asked Hughes to keep this information confidential. Sully handed Hughes a tough assignment.

"Here's the thing Howard. Although we are confident that the Guardians of Israel are responsible for both homicides, we don't know enough about them yet to go public. What I need from you is to find out if you guys have any Guardians living up here in Bakersfield. At the same, keep your inquires quiet. If we spook these guys, they'll go underground making our job of identifying them and putting them away near impossible."

Hughes acknowledged Sully and concurred with his concerns. It was late in the day when the Detectives wrapped things up at the Bakersfield Police Department and Sully was eager to get home. The drive back to Los Angeles was slow going. Traffic was heavy through the grapevine and of course, a jack-knifed big rig added to Sully's travel woes.

It was Friday morning and Sully had just sat down at his desk where he found a note from Bill Casey. The note related that Ricin had been confirmed as the cause of death in the murder of Ralph Doyle. Casey added that although he had stated earlier that he did not find any evidence that Detective Doyle had been beaten, he now needed to amend that report. Casey went on in the message to explain that he had now discovered that the suspects used a pair of pliers to crush Doyle's right testicle.

Sully recalled that Dr. Hastings' report had stated that each finger on the left hand of Amanda Cavanaugh had been broken with a pair of pliers. Sully thought, just more modus operandi to tie these two homicides together. Sully then began to imagine the crime that took place in Bakersfield. He placed the crime scene photos on his desk along with Hastings' report on the physical injuries sustained by Cavanaugh's body. Sully then began to create a chronology of events.

Amanda Cavanaugh is kidnapped by an unknown number of Skinheads belonging to the Guardians of Israel. She was driven to 1512 Maple Street in Bakersfield, California. Amanda was dragged into the abandoned house. Her hands and legs were bound with leather straps. Her body was suspended between two walls. Her clothing was cut away from her body leaving her hanging there nude. She was beaten and tortured in an apparent effort to extract information. Most likely the identity of her police contact and what exactly she had told him. Sully believed that Amanda would have been punched a few times in the torso to begin with. Followed by the breaking of the fingers of her left hand, prompting her to talk.

After learning what they wanted from Amanda, Sully imagined that it would be at this point that the right index finger would be amputated and used to write the words "Race Traitor" on the wall. Sully then had a visual picture of both crime scenes and realized that the words "Race Traitor" were written on the wall in view of the victim, allowing them to read the words that were written in their own blood.

Sully listed the branding as the next event. The Star of David had been burned into Amanda's chest. Then of course the tattoos would be burned from her body. Finally, Amanda would be beaten. Blows to her face would cause a fractured jaw and shattered cheek bone. Blunt blows to the head fracturing her skull in two places is most likely the injuries that ended her life.

The phone then rang. It was Detective Howard Hughes. Hughes related that Hastings had just informed him that he had confirmed the identity of the body as Amanda Cavanaugh. He added that the cause of death was a brain hemorrhage caused by the skull fractures. Sully related to Hughes that he had just learned that the suspects that murdered Detective Doyle also used a pair of pliers in a sadistic manner on him as well.

CHAPTER VI

GRIFFITH PARK

SULLY RETURNED HOME AT A DECENT HOUR FRIDAY. IN fact, Meg had not started to prepare dinner. As Sully parked his City car at the rear of the driveway, Meg came out to greet him. "Sully," she began, "you are not going to believe this! Captain Morton called me about fifteen minutes ago and told me that he had had me transferred to Major Crimes Division." It was unusual for a Reserve Officer to be assigned to work in a Division of the Department such as Major Crimes, especially in the Intelligence Sector. Meg had been putting in her two days a month working Newton Street patrol. Sully acknowledged, "I'll bet he wants you to start reviewing Doyle's investigation. All of his reports, notes, and anything else he might have in his files."

"Captain Morton thinks that I might be a big help to you in your investigation," Meg added. Sully followed with, "He's right you know. After all, I don't have the time to research the thousands of pages of intelligence reports that Ralph must have on these guys. Besides, with all he told you Sunday at the party, you're already ahead of me on this. All I can say is that I am glad that we will get a chance to finally do cop stuff together."

"I'm glad too," Meg stated. "I have always wanted to team up with you Sully. And, now that the time has come, I only wish that it was a reason other than Doyle's murder. Anyway, Captain Morton has asked me to work a couple of days a week instead of just two days a month. He said he would make it up to me somehow. Of course, I told him I would work as much as needed and I didn't expect him to make it up to me as I was doing it for Doyle," Meg ended.

Sully knew that Meg would be putting in a lot more than two days a week. Once she got into Doyle's files, she would be fixated and not want to put the work down. Sully inquired, "Have you talked to Clara about taking care of Shawn?" Meg told Sully, "Clara and Robert said they would come to our house to watch Shawn and also fix our meals." Sully nodded, while thinking to himself, Clara and Robert were possibly the best in-laws a man could hope to have. Sully enjoyed the company of Meg's sister and her brother-in-law, Robert. Sully felt that Robert cooked the best Bar-B-que in the greater Los Angeles area. Robert cooked steak to perfection. And, not only was he a master cook, he was good company. Robert enjoyed a good cigar and a bottle of beer as much as Sully.

The Sullivans turned in a little earlier than normal. No Jay Leno tonight. It had been a tough week on Sully. Perhaps the long hours on the interstate between Los Angeles and Bakersfield had taken in out of Sully. At any rate, it was lights out at 11:00 p.m. following the Fox News.

It was 7:30 Saturday morning when Sully began to stir. He reached an arm over to clutch onto Meg, but he found only her empty side of the bed. Sully then got a whiff of fresh brewed coffee, and then a hint of sizzling bacon. That was all he needed to be told it was now time to get up. Sully took care of his morning bathroom needs including splashing cold water on his face, and a quick brushing of his teeth. Sully threw on a bathrobe and headed to the kitchen. Meg pulled a chair out and had Sully sit down while she poured him a cup of coffee. Next came breakfast. Bacon with eggs, scrambled, with a little cheese thrown in, and rye toast. Meg sat down as well and the two ate while soaking up each other's smile.

The phone rang. Thankfully it was after Sully and Meg had finished their breakfast. It was Captain Stephanie Porter of Robbery Homicide Division. Captain Porter told Sully that they were investigating a homicide in Griffith Park that he should take a look at. Porter related that hikers had found the body this morning in the hills. Captain Porter told Sully that the nude body was suspended between two trees. She added that there was a fresh branded mark burned into the flesh of the deceased. Sully was instructed to report to the Ranger Station where he would be met by Detectives from Robbery Homicide.

It was 9:30 a.m. when Sully arrived at the Griffith Park Ranger Station. He was met by Detective Kathy Burgess. Sully knew Kathy, who had done some of her patrol time at Newton Street. Kathy greeted Sully and told him how sorry she was to learn about Ralph Doyle. She added, "I heard that you came up with another homicide in Bakersfield that may be connected." Sully told Kathy that he had been in Bakersfield on another homicide that he believes was committed by the same suspects. Sully didn't go into detail, reserving his thoughts and observations until after he examined the crime scene at hand. If he were to determine that this Griffith Park homicide was connected, well then, he would educate Kathy with what he had uncovered thus far.

Kathy grabbed Sully by the elbow as they were walking over to the four-wheel drive Ranger's vehicle. Stopping in their tracks, Kathy began to brief Sully. She told him that when she arrived this morning, she was told by the Park Ranger that this is the third such homicide that they have had her in the park. Kathy related that the victims are homosexuals. Kathy told Sully that the other two cases are a year and nine months old. Respectively, she said that they were given to Robbery Homicide because of the hate crime aspect. She told Sully that the Senior Detective working the case has been off for three months after suffering a heart attack. His partner retired last month, and the cases had not yet been re-assigned. So, when your teletype regarding Doyle was read, nobody made the connection.

Bill Clark, the Park Ranger, greeted Sully and then asked Kathy if this would be everyone. Kathy answered in the affirmative and the three began their drive through the park. The crime scene itself would be on a dirt trail on the hilltop. The ridgeline trails were a popular spot for homosexuals to sunbathe nude or just to frolic in the bushes together. Sully recalled during his tour of Vice at Newton Street; he was loaned to a Task Force put together to clean up the park that had become a heaven for bush orgies. Sully had spent several days working the park. The park spans 4,107 acres. It is the largest municipal park in the United States. There are fifty-three miles of bridle paths and hiking trails that wrap their way through the park's elevations that range from 384 to 1625 feet above sea level. Sully estimated another thirty miles of paved roadway winding their way through the park. The park was home to the Los Angeles Zoo, the Gene Autry Museum, Travel Town, the Los Angeles Observatory, and the Greek Theatre. The park was also home to kiddie rides, like the merry-go-round and pony rides, as well as, a first-class golf course for the adults.

As the three drove along the hillside road, Sully remembered traveling the roads in which every turn out was occupied by a gay male waiting to get hooked up. Sully grinned as he recalled Tarzan. At least that is what they dubbed him. Tarzan was a white male in his late fifties. He was very muscular, standing about five foot, ten inches. Tarzan would stretch his tanned body over the hood of his car wearing nothing more than a leopard swimsuit that looked more like an athletic supporter.

It was about a fifteen-minute drive from the Ranger Station to the crime scene. Bill Clark threw his Yukon in to four-wheel drive and turned off of the paved road and onto a fire break. It was an easy grade of about two hundred feet to the top of the ridge and it was another one hundred and fifty yards to a clump of trees. It would be in this area where the body of Gerald Grant would be found suspended between the trees.

Here again leather straps were tied to Gerald's wrists and ankles. His body was stretched out and suspended in mid air. His limbs were tied to the trees. The body was severely bruised from what must have been a brutal beating. Gerald's right ear had been cut off. Sully inquired, "Did anyone find a right ear nearby?" Bill answered, "No ear Detective. And you know that in the other two killings, each of those guys had their right ear cut off as well. Why would they do that? It's just weird!" "It's symbolic," Sully answered, "You see it's the right ear. Remember when men first began wearing earrings. There was an old saying, 'right ear queer, left ear Buccaneer'. These guys take the right ear of the queer as a trophy."

Sully walked a circle around the body looking at the ground for footprints and other markings that could be evidence. The entire area looked like it had been swept clean. Sully checked with Bill Clark, asking him if he had actually been at each of the homosexual crime scenes. Clark told Sully, "So far they all look the same. The bodies were all tied to trees in remote hilltop locations. No tire marks leading in or out of the area. All foot tracks swept away." Clark added, "Then there is the body, the burn marks and then the dildo." Sully questioned, "Dildo?" Clark answered, "Yeah, you mean no one told you? And, obviously you haven't looked." Again, Sully asked, "Look at what?" "His ass," answered Clark. Sully walked to the backside of Gerald Grant. There it was, the end of a dildo protruding from the rectum of the young Mr. Grant. Kathy then told sully that two previous victims were also found in this same manner. She advised him that the dildo's recovered were fifteen inches in length with a swastika carved into the head of the rubber penis.

Sully then focused his attention to the chest area of the victim. Here again our victim was branded. The brand in this case differed from that of Ralph Doyle and Amanda Cavanaugh. This brand was the symbol known to identify a hermaphrodite. The symbol is actually a blend of the male and female symbols. A circle with an arrow extending up from the upper right of the circle and a cross extending downward from the bottom of the circle.

It was 7:30 p.m. when Sully walked into the Homicide Room at Newton Street. Seated at his desk was Kathy Burgess, who greeted Sully with a big smile. Kathy had brought Sully the crime scene photos from the Gerald Grant homicide. Kathy also brought the photos and all related reports, including Coroner's reports, for the first two homicides in Griffith Park. The victims were: Richard Black, a male white, twenty-two years of age; and Peter Washington, a male black, nineteen years of age.

Along with the photographs and reports, Kathy also had the rap sheets for all three victims. The one thing Richard Black, Peter Washington and Gerald Grant had in common was that all three had numerous arrests for indecent exposure and lewd conduct. Acts which occurred right there in the Park. Sully sifted through the photographs of each crime scene. Each set of photos included several shots of the fifteen-inch dildo removed from the rectum of each of the victims. Sully examined the swastika carved into the head of each of the rather large rubber dicks. Sully looked up at Kathy. "Have you checked these things out? I mean, actually physically taken hold of them, and…." Kathy, her face read, and trying to hold back laughter said, "Come on Sully, a girl never tells!"

Sully continued, "No….No…. Look at these photos. Each one of these cocks has a perfect cut out of a swastika. I would like to actually look at them up close. I think these rubber dicks were actually molded with the swastika in them. I don't think they were carved in later. If this is the case, and we find the maker of the rubber pee pee, then we may be able to locate the pee pee purchaser."

All the while Sully was explaining his thoughts to Kathy, he was putting together a large three ring binder as a homicide book that would hold the reports and photographs for the murders of Black, Washington and Grant. Kathy gasped as Sully titled the homicide book "The Bush Family Killings." Sully looked up at Kathy. "Yeah, I know it lacks political correctness, but you have to admit it has originality and flair."

Sully invited Kathy to have a cup of coffee in the break room. While sipping on their hot joe, Sully asked Kathy if she would be interested in a trip to the Federal Building in West L.A. Sully could see the puzzlement in Kathy's eyes. He explained, "The FBI may have some information on a group of Skinheads that might very well be responsible for these homicides. Kathy informed Sully that she would welcome any direction in this case. She told Sully that not only did she get assigned the Grant case, but that she had also inherited the Black and Washington cases as well.

Sully asked Kathy to wait in the break room and enjoy her coffee while he made a call to Penny Adler at the Bureau and one to his wife, Meg. Kathy took a sip of her coffee and answered, "Take your time Sully." Sully first called Meg, who was spending her first day at Major Crimes Division. Sully wanted to know how she was doing. After all, the Anti-Terrorist Section there was reported to be awfully sterile. Everything there was either secret or confidential. Sully just didn't know how Meg was going to handle it. Meg assured

Sully that she was fine. Captain Morton sat her down at Doyle's desk and started her out with some generic intelligence reports on White Power ideology and stuff like that. She wouldn't get to the root of Doyle's investigation on the Guardians of Israel until sometime Tuesday afternoon. Meg then let Sully know that she'd gotten a lunch date her first twenty minutes in the office. She hesitated just a moment to allow Sully to stew, and then eased his pain by letting him know it was only Captain Morton.

Sully told Meg that he was taking Kathy Burgess out to the FBI to meet Penny Adler. Sully hoped that between the reports that Meg would read and the Intel he would get from Special Agent Adler, that they would make some headway with the investigation.

It was almost noon when Sully and Kathy arrived at 11000 Wilshire Blvd. The seventeen story Federal Building was home to the Los Angeles Division of the FBI. The FBI in Los Angeles was responsible for the counties of Los Angeles, Orange, San Bernardino, Riverside, Ventura, Santa Barbara, and San Luis Obispo. Some 800 agents were assigned to the Los Angeles Division. Not all worked at the Wilshire location. Resident Agencies were set up in outlying areas. In fact, the Santa Ana R.A., as it was called, had more agents assigned to it than some other divisions of the FBI.

Special Agent Adler met the detectives on the steps of the Federal Building. Sully made the introductions between Adler and Burgess. This was followed by the most important decision of the day. Where to do lunch? Fish and chips in Santa Monica was the winning choice. On the drive to the oceanfront restaurant, Penny suggested that they spend the afternoon in her office reviewing what she had on the Guardians of Israel. She admitted that she did not have a lot. But that what she did have could be finished up with by Tuesday afternoon. Penny then added that Doyle's funeral would be all day Wednesday. Penny thought that the three of them could meet her source possibly Thursday. That is, if she could get permission from her supervisor. The FBI was very good about guarding the identity of their assets. It was actually a good practice after all. The fewer people that knew the identity of an informant, the safer the informant would be.

CHAPTER VII

THE FUNERAL

T HE FUNERAL COMMEMORATING THE LIFE OF A POLICE
Officer killed in the line of duty is like no other. It is filled with
pomp and circumstance, as well as, traditions handed down
from one generation of law enforcement to another. At almost every
police officer funeral you will find the bagpipers, a rider-less horse,
a helicopter flyover with a missing man formation and concluded by
taps and the traditional twenty-one-gun salute. Police funerals are
attended by uniformed police officers from neighboring agencies of
the fallen officer. Then there are those funerals that draw worldwide
attention. In the case of the four California Highway Patrol officers
gunned down in the Newhall Area of Los Angeles County, law
enforcement officers from as far away as England attended the
services.

Ralph Doyle's funeral was one for the record books. The
services took place eleven days following his murder. It was a cloudy
Wednesday morning when police officers began arriving at the Los
Angeles Catholic Arch Diocese in downtown Los Angeles. The
Cardinal himself would preside over the services.

Doyle, an Irish Catholic, would himself have scoffed at the
hypocrisy of it all. Doyle, although Catholic and a true believer
in God and the hereafter, was not a true church person. If you
posed the ultimate question to Doyle, "When is the last time you

saw the inside of a confessional?" Doyle would surely be at a loss
for words, stammering and stuttering for an answer. But the fact is,
Doyle really merited this funeral and all the accolades that would be
bestowed upon him during the eulogy.

Under normal circumstances, a funeral for a fallen officer
would take place within a week of the officer's death. In Doyle's
case however, there were two key issues that caused the delay. First,
of course, was the cause of death. Bill Casey at the Los Angeles
Coroner's office needed to prove his theory that Ricin was the cause
of death in the Doyle case. The other issue that delayed scheduling
a funeral date was due to the hundreds of inquiries from law
enforcement agencies spanning the globe. There were a multitude
of agencies expressing a desire to send honor guards to assist and
stand side by side with their brothers and sisters wearing the badge
of L.A.P.D.

Doyle had been assigned to Intelligence for the better part of his
forty-two-year career. For the most part, his Domestic Terrorism
investigations were related to the White Supremacist Groups. Doyle
belonged to many intelligence sharing organizations. L.E.I.U. (Law
Enforcement Intelligent Unit) was one the finest member agencies.
Its membership included law enforcement agencies spanning across
the United States representing various state and local police officers.
Most federal law enforcement agencies were represented as well.
L.E.I.U. strived to protect American citizens from the evil acts of
terrorists, as well as, protecting against the criminal endeavors of
organized crime. All this was done, while enforcing the United
States Constitution and the rights given to each of our citizens of
free speech and the ability to assemble in protest.

Doyle's involvement in these organizations put him into contact
with law enforcement officers throughout the United States. He also
made contacts in far reaching locations around the globe. So, it
was no wonder when these agencies expressed an interest in being
represented at Doyle's funeral.

Sully and Meg both arrived at the Arch Diocese in their
Class A uniforms. It was normal for Detectives to attend a police
officer's funeral in a dark suit. But Sully wanted to honor his friend
by joining with all the uniformed officers representing so many

police agencies. Temple Street had been closed between Hope Street and Los Angeles Street for the parking of the police cars that were driven by the police officers attending the services. It was still early. There was a good hour and a half before the uniformed contingent would be ordered to attention and march into the Cathedral. Sully began to scan the growing crowd of uniforms. The usual uniforms from Los Angeles County Police Agencies were present. Hundreds of them could be seen. Most were those of the L.A.P.D. and the Los Angeles Sheriff's Department. There also were large groups of uniformed officers representing their agencies from as far south as San Diego and as far north as Sacrament. Sully nudged Meg with an elbow and pointed out four uniformed officers from the Honolulu Police Department talking with a group of officers from the San Francisco Police Department.

Out of state police agencies included New York, New Jersey, Chicago, Dallas, Oklahoma, Spokane, Seattle, Portland, Coeur d'Alene and Las Vegas. More impressive thought Sully was the attendance of the international police agencies. Royal Canadian mounted police sent a contingent of fifteen uniformed officers. The Australian Federal Police and the Israeli National Police organizations also had a uniformed presence.

Sully had always known of Doyle's work in the field of White Power, but he had not known that Doyle had also worked many years investigating the Jewish Defense League, a violent group forged in the late 1960's. The JDL, as it was commonly called, began as the Protectors of the Jewish community merchants from the street thugs that had moved in. Later, the group evolved into Nazi hunters and Arab haters. In the 1970's they focused their attentions to the plight of Soviet Jews and actually carried out a campaign of terror aimed at the Soviet Mission to the United Nations.

Doyle's relationship with the Israeli National Police stemmed from inquiries by the Israeli authorities regarding the immigration of young American Jews with ties to the JDL to the West Bank area. In fact, in all the years that Sully knew Doyle and all that they had talked about, Doyle never once mentioned to Sully that he had spent two weeks in Israel on an investigation. Sully was realizing that there was a lot about his old buddy's work that he would never know.

It was nearing time to enter the Cathedral. Sully took a quick glance up and down Temple Street. Four city blocks of police cars were parked six abreast. A corps of fifteen bagpipers and six drummers, two of which beat on large base drums, warmed up off to the side.

Sully estimated the uniformed presence to be between sixteen and eighteen hundred. Non-uniformed law enforcement easily amounted to another eight hundred. About three hundred and fifty of these were FBI Agents from Los Angeles, San Francisco, San Diego, Las Vegas and Salt Lake City. The highest-ranking FBI Agent was the Assistant Director in Charge, (ADIC), of Los Angeles. As Sully and Meg began to line up with the company of uniformed officers he noticed Special Agent Penny Adler in the crowd of FBI Agents. Penny also noticed Sully and gave a little wave, and then a gesture, as if to say, "I need to talk to you." Sully nodded signaling that he understood.

The group of uniformed officers was called to attention. The bagpiper and drum corps began to play, and the officers began to march single file into the Cathedral. It was almost thirty-five minutes before the hollowed halls were full. Several hundred people were left out in the patio area to listen on speakers set up for the expected overflowing crowd.

Standing before the flower filled altar was the flag draped coffin of Detective Ralph Doyle. The pew normally set aside for family, was instead filled with dignitaries. Doyle, a widower, had long ago buried his parents. Doyle had no brothers or sisters and his only marriage in life bore him one son, Bryan. Bryan, who was close to his father, chose a career in the United States Marine Corps. Gunnery Sergeant Bryan Doyle was killed in Desert Storm. So an extended family consisting of the Chief of Police, Captain Morton, the Mayor of Los Angeles, the Governor of the State of California, the Assistant Director in Charge of the Los Angeles Division of the FBI and the Los Angeles Police Chaplain occupied the pew.

The Cardinal of the Los Angeles Diocese opened with a prayer. He then went on to explain that a traditional Catholic funeral would include Mass with Holy Communion. He conceded that to follow along with the Catholic tradition would extend this service well into next week. The Cardinal agreed that following a more traditional police service would be the best avenue to honor Ralph Doyle's soul and perpetuate it on its journey to the Heavens to be with God.

The Cardinal spoke of Doyle's time on this earth and how he served God as one of his Centurions. He spoke of how Doyle had been married in the Catholic Church and had chose to raise his son, Bryan, in the Catholic faith. He added that Bryan gave his life, as did his father, by serving God, in the protection of others who were unable to defend themselves of the evils sponsored by Satan.

The Chief spoke next. He praised Doyle for his efforts to protect the citizens of Los Angeles from the violence that accompanies terrorism. The Chief assured those attending that Doyle had died for a cause he firmly believed in. That cause was a life in the City of Los Angeles free of hate driven terror. He assured the audience that Doyle's death would not go unavenged. The Chief looked up toward the heavens and thanked Doyle for his dedication and sacrifice. He added that the Department would miss him, the City would miss him, and the Law Enforcement Community would surely miss him. The Chief closed by simply stating, "God Bless you Ralph Doyle."

Captain Morton began his eulogy of Detective Doyle: "He was born Ralph Eugene O'Doyle in Dublin Ireland to Eugene and Katherine O'Doyle. Ralph, at the age of three moved to Los Angeles, California with his parents. The "O" in his name was obviously lost in the American translation and Ralph Doyle began his American Dream. Doyle joined the Los Angeles Police Department in August 1964, one year before the City erupted in rioting. Doyle took Anna Marie O'Toole as his bride on January 18, 1969. Bryan Eugene Doyle arrived a few short years later and was the pride of the Doyle lineage. Anna Marie passed on while Bryan was still in his formative years. Doyle, a single father, poured his heart and soul into the task of raising Bryan, a responsibility that he did not take lightly.

Bryan, after completing High School, joined the United States Marine Corps. Bryan achieved the rank of Gunnery Sergeant, while at the same time completing a Bachelor's Degree. Bryan had been accepted to Officer Candidate School prior to being deployed during Desert Storm. Bryan Eugene Doyle was killed in action; an event that greatly impacted the life of Detective Ralph Doyle. Still today on Doyle's desk at work you will find Bryan's Purple heart proudly displayed in a case Doyle made with his own hands."

Captain Morton went on to address all the accomplishments that spanned Doyle's police career. These included awards and the commendations Doyle had received from the Department, the FBI, the United States Secret Service and so many other law enforcement agencies, and citizens alike.

The Captain then began to show his anger over the murder of his Senior Detective. Morton explained that Doyle had been brutally murdered by the very degenerate Neo-Nazi Skinheads that he was currently investigating.

"A 'Race Trader' is what they dubbed him!" Morton exclaimed, his voice trembling, but with fire in his words. Morton continued, "How can a man be a traitor to his race when he strives to see his race live and prosper through co-existence with other peoples?"

Morton, his face now red with anger and his eyes tearing apologized for letting his emotions get out of control. To his surprise the Cathedral echoed with a very loud round of applause. Captain Morton walked over to the flag draped coffin and placed his right hand on it. "Dear friend, we have all come together here today to see you off on your journey to join Anna Marie and Bryan Eugene. We thank you for your friendship, your dedication and your leadership. May God bless you Ralph Eugene Doyle," Martin closed.

Sergeant Anthony Donatello, the Department's Chaplain, gave a final prayer after which the honor guard approached the altar from the rear of the Cathedral. Kimberly Williams, a young female officer stood at the altar and sang "Did you ever know that you're my hero?" A song that brought a tear to every eye, opened or closed. After the song, the pipers began to play as they escorted Doyle's flag draped coffin out to the awaiting hearse.

The processional stretched for miles with nearly one thousand marked police vehicles with light bars lit up. Several hundred unmarked police vehicles with red dash lights as well, were glowing through the windshields. Add in all the civilian cars and you have a traffic nightmare for a motorist just trying to get from Point A to Point B. No matter the inconvenience, there were many Angelenos standing at the side of their cars and held their right hand over their hearts as the hearse passed slowly by honoring one of Los Angeles' fallen heroes.

The hearse arrived at an area of Forest Lawn, Hollywood Hills, just beside the Old North Church. The pallbearers assembled as did the bagpipe and drum corps. Little did either know that it would be another thirty-five minutes before everyone arrived at graveside. The rider-less horse was standing in place draped with a black blanket over its saddle with the initials L.A.P.D. at its bottom edge. A lone bugler stood on a nearby knoll. A squad of riflemen stood at parade rest awaiting their orders to fire the twenty-one-gun salute.

The grave itself was overshadowed by the American Patriotic mural depicting the American Revolution. Doyle would be laid to rest between Anna Marie and Bryan Eugene. His parents' final resting site was nearby as well.

The bagpipes and drums began to play "Amazing Grace" as the pallbearers moved Doyle's casket toward the gravesite. After setting the casket down, the pallbearers stepped back two paces. This allowing room for the honor guard to move in and remove the flag from the coffin. The flag was folded and presented to Captain Morton, as Doyle was not survived by a family member. Captain Morton intended to encase the flag and hang it and Bryan's Purpleheart in the squad room at Major Crimes Division. After Morton took possession of the flag, following the military-like ritual, the honor guard again stepped up to the casket. They were then marched away by their Detail Leader.

The Cardinal, now dressed in a black officiating robe with a red sash belt and red cap, gave the final prayer as the crowd responded in unison "Amen." The police helicopters flew overhead in missing man formation, the rifles rang out in a twenty-one-gun salute and "Taps" was played by the bugler.

As the group began to break up, Sully saw Bill Casey from the Coroner's office. Sully was shocked to see Casey dressed in a very expensive looking black suit. Casey was seldom ever seen in a suit and, in fact, almost everything he normally wore looked kind of frumpy like he had picked it up at a Thrift store. Sully acknowledged Casey stating, "Bill, nice of you to attend. Did you know Ralph?" Casey replied, "No, I never had the opportunity to work with Detective Doyle. It's just that since I started working at the Coroner's office, I have attended the funeral services of every police officer killed in Los Angeles County." Casey added, "And, there's been way too many to count!"

Sully was somewhat surprised. He thought it noble of Casey to honor these officers but, at the same time, thought how depressing it must be. "You know Bill, that's really a tribute to the type of guy you are. I know cops that refuse to go to police funerals because they are just to heart wrenching. I think that the fact that you put yourself through this time and again to honor these guys, speaks well of your persona," Sully told Bill Casey.

"You know Sully, I finished Medical School along with a bunch of other courses, to become a Medical Examiner. I think I'm a smart guy but sometimes, when they start using words that I need a dictionary for...well, I just throw up my arms and say to myself, "Fuck it! I guess that's a compliment!" Casey then turned and walked off.

Penny Adler then approached Sully. Penny told Sully that she found some additional reports that she got from Doyle's files on the Skinhead case. Penny told Sully that she talked to her supervisor about disclosing the source's identity. Penny explained that her supervisor got concurrence from the United States Attorney's office. "So, we are good to go tomorrow," Penny stated.

CHAPTER VIII

THE INFORMANT

I T WAS 7 A.M. WHEN SULLY AND KATHY TEAMED UP with Penny on Thursday morning at the Federal Building. Penny remarked about Doyle's funeral and what a great tribute it was to his career with the L.A.P.D. Sully agreed that it was a hero's send off. Sully told the two women that he and his wife along, with a handful of Doyle's close professional friends, remained at the gravesite until Doyle's casket was in the ground and covered with dirt and topped with sod.

Sully told them that an old timer, an Academy classmate of Ralph's, Anthony Flemming, was one of those that stayed back. Sully told them that Lieutenant Flemming had told him that he had submitted his retirement papers the week before Doyle was murdered. Yesterday, before the funeral, he walked into Personnel and pulled his papers. He told Sully that he would not retire until those responsible were arrested, Sully added.

He told me that his gang unit is on standby. He grabbed my arm and stared into my eyes, seemingly through my eyes and said, "You understand?" Man, talk about an eerie feeling. Well, I looked right back at him and said, "Yeah. I understand. You want to be there." He let go of my arm said, "Thanks." Then he walked over and placed a single red rose on Doyle's grave.

Sully could tell that the girls were touched by his tale of events. Penny then began to relate her knowledge of the informant. Penny admitted that she was given the informant only six weeks ago but that she had read his file to bring herself up to speed.

Sully was behind the wheel and was about ready to exit the Federal Building property on to Sepulveda. Sully interrupted Penny to get directions as he inquired, "Which way?" Penny laughed and replied, "I guess that would be an important bit of intell. My guy lives in Fallbrook."

Sully headed south on the 405 freeway. Fallbrook was in North San Diego County at the rear of the United States Marine Corps Base Camp at Pendleton. As they drove, Penny continued to brief Sully and Kathy. The guys name is Richard Reinstadt. He is obviously male, white. He is sixty-three years old. The guy is maybe five foot six inches and physically fit.

"Short-man's-syndrome?" Sully asked. "File reads like it." Penny answered.

Penny continued, "The guy has been involved in almost every movement in the Extreme Right. He has been a member of the Ku Klux Klan, the Aryan Nations, the National Alliance, the White Aryan Resistance and the California Militia."

Sully interrupted, "Without specifics, has he ever given you anything worthwhile?" Penny told Sully that the informant has provided mostly literature distributed by the various groups. She added that he had also, in the past, provided partial membership lists. Penny reminded Sully that she had just been given the source six week earlier.

Sully followed up with another question. "Who had Richard before you?" Penny explained that Reinstadt had been in the Spokane, Washington area working with the FBI there on a Militia matter.

It was not unusual for one FBI Division to loan one of its sources to an office out of state. It was always easier and faster to infiltrate an organization with someone already established in like organizations. It was also safer for the investigation to use someone that was already tested and reliable than it was to recruit and cultivate a subject of the group under investigation. Penny told the pair that she had only actually had face to face contact with him one time. The Agent that had handled Reinstadt before went to Washington and retired about eight months ago.

With traffic it took the three two and a half hours to get to Fallbrook. Penny had arranged the meeting with Reinstadt to take place in a remote area of a rather large City park. As they pulled into the parking lot of a secluded area of the park, Sully noted only one other vehicle parked there. It was a faded blue 1999 oldsmobile 98. There were a variety of bumper stickers on the rear of the car. "Hitler Was Right" and "The Klan Wants You!" The later one had a hooded klansman pointing his finger. A take off obviously of the "Uncle Sam Wants You" recruitment posters. A couple of other stickers read "White Pride Worldwide" and the other simply read, "Fourteen Words." Sully made a mental note. After all, he could figure out what the other bumper stickers meant, it was "Fourteen Words" that had him stumped. Sully knew Special Agent Adler would be able to explain it to him.

Penny made the introductions, "Richard Reinstadt, this is Detective William Sullivan and his partner, Kathy Burgess, of the Los Angeles Police Department." She went on, "Detectives this is Richard." After the usual handshakes and pleasantries, the group sat down at a picnic table. Sully began, "I am told that you have had extensive contact with White Supremacist Groups for several years." Richard responded, "Actually, the better part of my life has been spent as an activist in the Extreme Right-Wing Ideology. My father took me to my first Klan meeting when I was just fifteen years old. It was the Mississippi Knights of the Ku Klux Klan. There I saw my first cross lighting."

Sully followed up with, "I understand that you have had experience with a variety of White Supremacist organizations. Have you had any contact with Neo-Nazi Skinheads in Los Angeles?" Richard Reinstadt paused, and then looked at Sully with his arms folded on the table. "Do these skinheads have a name? You know, like Hamerskins, or I don't know maybe American Front? Something like that? Do you have any individual skinhead in mind? You know, a key suspect?"

Sully didn't hesitate. He immediately answered, "No." Sully didn't want to give Penny or Kathy an opening to admit that they were in fact looking at the Guardians of Israel. Sully had a very uncomfortable feeling about Richard Reinstadt. Sully felt that Reinstadt was attempting to interrogate him to learn exactly what he might know. Sully added, "Actually Richard, we are at a loss in the investigation. Our Detective was murdered in his home. The words 'Race Traitor' were written on the wall. The Detective worked Intelligence and it was his job to monitor White Supremacist Groups. We just naturally thought that he was killed because of his work. In Los Angeles we don't have organized movements such as The Klan, so we just naturally assumed a group of Neo-Nazi Skinheads may be responsible."

Richard nodded, "I see. Looks like you have a real 'who done it' on your hands. Tell me. Have you been able to link this murder to any others?" Again, Sully was quick to respond. "No. And you know you would think that there would be additional Race Traitor executions like this."

Sully was now very suspicious of Reinstadt. He did not care if he was a tested informant or source, as the FBI would call him. Sully felt that Reinstadt was trying to determine if the murder of Doyle had been linked to the murder of the gays in Griffith Park. What's more, was Reinstadt trying to find out if the police had located the body of Amanda Cavanaugh and establish the connection to Doyle? At the same time that Sully's suspicions peaked regarding Reinstadt, he didn't want Reinstadt to put up his guard. Sully stated, "You know Richard, we may be able to utilize your exceptional services. Penny has told us that you have only been back in the area for a couple of months now. And, that you were out of state for the past year."

"Year and a half," Reinstadt corrected the Detective. "Yes. A year and a half," Sully repeated. At any rate, a guy of your caliber, a guy like you, that has been so active in the Movement. Well, I am confident that you could be of great assistance. I think it best that we don't meet again. We should do everything through Agent Adler. Do you agree?"

Richard enthusiastically replied, "You can count on me. I'll start putting out feelers today." As they all stood up, Sully reached out and shook Richard's hand and said, "Thank you Sir. We can use all the help you can give us." Richard nodded. He moved his hand from Sully's and shook hands with Kathy and nodded. Richard then shook hands with Penny and stated, "Agent Adler. I'll get on this right away and I'll be in touch with you."

They waited as Richard Reinstadt drove out of the park. Sully turned and looked at Penny and Kathy and explained. "I don't trust this guy. He was attempting to interrogate me. He wants to know exactly what we already know about the Guardian of Israel. Tell me something Penny. And don't get me wrong. I don't want to offend anyone, but I need to know what happened in the Spokane investigation?" Sully admitted to the pair that he was lost in the realm of intelligence. It was a beast he wanted no part of. Sully did explain that over the years he had dealt with the very same run-of-the-mill informants and his experience, as well as his gut, told him something was out of sorts with Richard Reinstadt. Penny really lacked the personal experience with Richard to have seen something amiss before Sully had pointed it out. Penny told Sully that she could see where he was going with this. And that she agreed with his conclusion. She admitted that she trusted Richard unconditionally because he had been an established source for several years. None of the Agents that handled cases with him in the past had ever questioned his loyalty. But what Penny didn't have for Sully was an answer to his question as to what happened in Spokane.

Penny suggested that they drive back up the Interstate somewhere and stop for lunch. She said that when they stopped, she would call the office on a hard wire phone and check out the Spokane case. On the drive north looking for a place to stop for lunch, Sully questioned Penny about the bumper sticker. "Fourteen Words. What does it mean?" Penny explained that "Fourteen Words" was a battle cry for Skinhead groups. She added that other groups refer to the words as well, but that the "Fourteen Words" were more popular with the Skinhead Movement. Penny then recited the words from memory. "We must secure the existence of our people and a future for white children."

They stopped at a Mexican Restaurant just down the street from the Mission at San Juan Capistrano. Sully and Kathy dug in and began enjoying the chips and salsa while Penny made her call to her office. She ended her call and returned to the table just as they were replacing the empty basket of chips and empty bowls of salsa. Penny sat down and shook her head. "Hey guys. I'm sorry," she told them. It was a big mistake to think Richard Reinstadt was going to give us the brass ring. "Sully." She explained, "You pegged this guy. He may just be trying to pump us for information like you said. The Spokane case was a bust. The investigation there spanned two years. Spokane inserted an Undercover Agent into the Group just before Richard was sent up there. About three months ago the Militia challenged the Agent, telling him that they knew he was an FBI Agent from Salt Lake City." Penny continued, "The Agent was assigned to Salt Lake and loaned to Spokane specifically for that case. Richard, a couple of weeks later, claimed that members of the Militia had begun to look at him with unusual scrutiny. He told the Agents that he felt his life was in danger. He suggested that he tell the Militia members that he did not feel comfortable now that the FBI had been able to compromise them. And, he intended to return to California."

Penny explained that the Agents felt that this excuse would work to not only get Reinstadt out of the Militia but protect his reputation as well continuing his value as a source." Penny then added, "The Salt Lake City Agent said in a debriefing that about seven months before he was challenged by the Militia, Richard Reinstadt had manipulated him in a conversation in which he told Richard that his family was at home in Salt Lake City."

Sully responded, "We need a game plan for Mr. Reinstadt." Sully looked at Penny. "He is your source. Do you think your people can put him under surveillance? I don't know if you could get a Title III, but I'm sure you could get a pen register and do a mail stop. It's your call Penny."

Penny agreed and told Sully that she would get on it when she got back to her office. Lunch was placed in front of them and not another word was uttered at lunch. There really wasn't any conversation after lunch either. Oh, there were a few moans and groans from the three who had overeaten but the drive back to Los Angeles was peaceful. Sully drove while both Kathy and Penny napped in the car.

CHAPTER IX

FOLLOW THE LEADER

T WAS 6:30 PM WHEN SULLY ARRIVED HOME. MEG WAS IN the kitchen putting the finishing touches on a chicken Caesar's salad. A simple, but healthy dinner with one possible exception, the dressing. As Sully entered through the door, Meg pulled a long neck Silver Bullet from the refrigerator to greet him with.

As Sully took a hearty drink of the cold beer, Meg began to explain her day at the office. She began by telling Sully that she has been partnered with Lieutenant Anthony Flemming. Sully already knew that Flemming had pulled his retirement papers and vowed to stay with the Department until the murder of Doyle was solved. Flemming had also remarked to Sully that he wanted to be involved in the arrest of those responsible. The thing that Sully did not know was that this Old Salt of a street gunfighter had walked into the Chief's office and handed the Chief his transfer to Major Crimes Division. Flemming typed up his own transfer never consulting with his Captain at Newton Street and without the permission of Captain Morton. Sully learned later that Flemming had walked up and stood in front of the Chief's desk handing the Chief his transfer. Flemming simply stated, "Chief, here is my transfer to Major Crimes Division. I'm going to be there until my retirement. Which will be the day after I assist in the arrest of those degenerate goose- stepping, Hitler worshiping assholes. Now, you may as well sign the papers because I'm going to be in this investigation one way or the other."

The Chief sat there quietly and took in every word that Flemming had to say. After the Lieutenant had his say, the Chief picked up the transfer papers and looked them over. He then sat them down on the desk in front of him as he looked up at Anthony Flemming.

As he signed the order, he stated, "These documents look like they are in order Lieutenant. Welcome to the Major Crimes Division."

Lieutenant Flemming accepted the papers from the Chief and thanked him as he turned to leave. Just as Flemming reached the office doorway, the Chief spoke up. "Lieutenant. I am confident that this transfer is purely for professional reasons and not for reasons of revenge, because if I thought that you were one of those cops that would let emotion cloud his judgment… If I thought that you were one of those cops that would compromise his values and the values of the Department… Well, it would be retirement papers and not transfer papers being signed here today. Do we have an understanding?"

"Yes Sir Chief. We do." With that said Flemming left the Chief's office.

Meg told Sully that when she first got to the offices of Major Crimes Division she was greeted by Captain Morton who escorted her into his office. Seated at a round table in the office was Anthony Flemming. Atop the table was a stack of files. Meg sat down, smiled and shook hands with Flemming. Meg didn't think it was odd to find Flemming seated there. After all, he was a Police Lieutenant. And, as far as she knew, he was just possibly the most senior member of the L.A.P.D. Meg knew too that Flemming and Doyle had been classmates at the Police Academy.

Meg related that she and Lieutenant Flemming spent the day reading the files that Doyle had compiled on the Guardians of Israel. Meg told Sully, "If there is one thing my gut tells me, it's that there is not one leader in the bunch!"

Meg went on to relate to Sully that she and Tony, a nickname she had given to Lieutenant Anthony Flemming, had read each of the files and none of the intelligence reports reflected that anyone of the skinheads was capable of organizing a sock drawer, much less a movement. Meg told Sully that Justin Davis, who Doyle named as the Group's Leader, didn't have the where withal to plan a murder.

Sully had great respect for Meg's analytical perception or intuitiveness. Sully felt there was something to be said for a woman's intuition. Even Sully's first wife was very astute when it came to woman's intuition. That's the thing that he admired about her. In fact, there were two things that he admired about his first wife. The second was the way her mouth knew its way around his manhood.

Sully told Meg as they sat down to enjoy their salad, that he agreed with her assessment of the group. In between bites, Sully explained that he had met with an FBI source earlier in the day and felt that the source may somehow be involved with the skinhead group. Sully explained that he had a gut feeling with this guy, and in fact, if he were female it would be a classic case of woman's intuition.

Meg interrupted, "Can you tell me about him?"

"Sure," Sully answered. "He is a little man in his mid- sixties. One of those kind of guys with the short man's syndrome. He has been involved since age fifteen starting with the Ku Klux Klan. He even has a German name, Richard Reinstadt."

"Oh shit Sully!" Meg interrupted. "I read that name today in one of Ralph's reports!"

"Are you sure?" Questioned Sully.

"Sure I'm sure. Are you kidding? A name like Reinstadt jumps right out at you." Meg assured, "Doyle interviewed him."

Sully, not quite done with his chicken Caesar salad put dinner on hold while he called Agent Adler on his cell phone. While waiting for her to answer, Sully asked Meg if the report she read had reflected the date that Doyle had talked to Reinstadt. Meg told Sully that she wasn't sure and that she didn't actually read the report. Reinstadt's file was the last one that they saw. Meg told Sully that it appeared to be a rather lengthy interview and that she and Tony had left it for tomorrow to finish.

Penny Adler responded to the ring of her cell phone.

"This is Agent Adler."

"Good evening Penny. This is Sully. Sorry to be a pest. I know you're on your own time now and probably in the middle of dinner, but I couldn't wait until tomorrow to ask you something about Doyle."

"First of all, you don't need to apologize for interrupting my dinner. Believe me, it's nothing to write home about. So, let's get to your question," Penny requested.

"Do you know that Ralph Doyle interviewed Richard Reinstadt?" Sullly asked.

"No, I did not know that. Do you know when it was that Doyle talked to Reinstadt?" Penny questioned.

"No. I really don't know much as yet. My wife has been reviewing Doyle's files on the Guardians of Israel and came across a file with a lengthy intelligence interview with Reinstadt. We hope to go through it in great depth in the morning. I just wanted to know if you were aware of the interview." Sully explained.

"No. But I would appreciate it if you would fill me in on the details after you have had a chance to digest things." Penny requested.

Sully assured Agent Adler that he would fill her in on the details of Doyle's interview and offered to supply her with a copy of Doyle's file. Sully then rejoined Meg at the table and completed his dinner. Sully told Meg that he would go by Robbery Homicide Division in the morning and pick up Kathy Burgess and then meet up with Meg and Lieutenant Anthony Flemming. Sully couldn't bring himself to call him Tony as Meg did. Sully asked Meg to make four Xerox copies of the interview Doyle conducted with Reinstadt.

Meg had made a pot of coffee for after dinner. After pouring a cup for herself and Sully, she made a quick call to her Sister Clara to check on young Shawn Patrick. Clara put Meg's mind at ease by telling her that little Shawn was having a grand time at Aunt Clara and Uncle Robert's house. Meg was relieved that Shawn was doing just fine, but it didn't prevent her from being a little sad and lonely without him home.

Sully could see the sadness in Meg's face when she came into the family room. Sully reached out to Meg and guided her to the sofa. Sully pulled Meg to him and snuggled.

"Miss the little guy, don't you?" He asked. "Me too." Sully added.

"Thank God he'll be home tomorrow when we get off work." Meg said with a smile.

Sully thought perhaps they could take advantage of the fact that they were alone in the house. Sully invited Meg for a hot shower.

Meg eagerly accepted. As the two stepped into the shower, the hot water was already steaming up the bathroom. However, before Sully and Meg would step out of the shower, they would do some steaming up action of their own.

Sully and Meg took turns lathering and washing each other. It was a sensual, massage-like washing. Neither one skipped an area of the other's body, prolonging the shower. Along with the sudsy caresses of each other's body parts, were several lavish kisses. By the time the two emerged from the steam filled shower, there was no detouring what was to follow.

After toweling each other off, Sully laid down on the bed. Meg crawled in next to him and immediately began kissing Sully first on his chest and then down his stomach to his navel where she made circular motions with her tongue, penetrating his belly button. Meg moved her head and tongue further down Sully's belly to the head of his erect penis that was resting on his stomach just below his navel. Meg began teasing the area commonly called the "Fireman's helmet" with her tongue. After a few moments of this playful frolicking Meg took Sully into her mouth and began copulating him with great passion. It was as if Meg was getting turned on as much as Sully was by Meg's erotic performance.

Sully allowed Meg to please him orally for several moments. Almost to the point where he would lose control. Sully, wanting to continue in the moment, rolled Meg over on her back freeing himself from her mouth. Sully began kissing Meg passionately. First kissing her on the mouth and then down her neck. Sully reached her breasts and began taking a nipple into his mouth gently sucking on one and then alternating to the other. Sully would suck on the nipple briefly and then sweep a circle around it with his tongue. Sully lingered at her breasts for several minutes before his tongue continued its journey downward to Meg's honey pot. Sully took Meg's clitoris between his lips and gently sucked on it. Sully then circled Meg's clit with his tongue. Meg's juices were already flowing with excitement, but these added sensations were peaking her sexual excitement.

Sully gave pause to Meg's clitoris attempting to delay her orgasm while his tongue explored other regions of her womanhood.

Sully inserted his tongue into Meg's vagina swirling it around. His tongue circled her urethra and then sucked her labia minora area in between his lips while taunting them with his tongue. Sully returned his attention to her clitoris which was now fully erect and throbbing. It was only seconds after Sully re-directed his efforts at Meg's clit until she reached an orgasm and pulled away from Sully. Her clitoris now very sensitive.

Meg, now wanting to take control, rolled Sully over onto his back. Meg climbed on top of Sully and slid him into her. Meg began sliding up and down, plunging Sully deep inside her. Meg panting, almost out of breath, rode Sully wildly. Just as Sully thought he couldn't take any more, Meg stopped the vigorous plunging. She arched her back and began grinding her pelvis into his. Sully reached up and cupped her breasts. Sully could see her nipples hard and erect. Even the tiny bumps at the edge of the areolas were hard. Sully compared Meg's nipples to those of a woman stepping out of a cold pool. But as Sully noted there was no chill in their bedroom. One would have accredited this to be the result of sexual arousement.

Meg's grinding became more intense. She began to moan with pleasure. Sully too was being overpowered by the funny feeling and he too began to breathe heavily and began thrusting himself deeply into Meg with fast, powerful strokes. The two continued gasping in unison and uttering sounds of pleasure; grinding and thrusting at each other faster and faster to the point of complete satisfaction. Sully thrust himself completely into Meg and held himself in as deep as possible while he exploded. He then pulled back and thrust himself deeply once again discharging a second burst of his hot juices. One last deep thrust would drain him. Meg too was spent. She laid there on top of Sully for several minutes. Meg would not roll off of Sully until his flaccid penis slid out of her.

They both enjoyed a very somber and rewarding sleep. Awakening revitalized on Friday morning Sully was first to shower and dress. He prepared a breakfast of fresh fruit and a slice of toast, as well as, a hot cup of coffee. After they enjoyed the final sip, it was off to work for the two of them. Only one slight change in the plans though. Kathy Burgess had called while Sully was in the shower.

She told Meg that she did not need Sully to pick her up at Robbery Homicide Division. She would meet them at Major Crimes Division at 8 a.m.

As Sully and Meg arrived and parked in the underground parking lot, Kathy Burgess was just pulling into the parking garage as well. The three entered Major Crimes together and found Lieutenant Flemming at the Xerox machine making copies of Doyle's report on Richard Reinstadt. The group was met by Captain Morton, who led them into his office. Morton told the four that his office would give them more privacy. Additionally, he pointed out that he had set up a coffeemaker for them along with some bite size muffins.

Captain Morton left the office and they settled down to business. From reading Doyle's report, it was clear that Ralph Doyle had no previous knowledge of Richard Reinstadt. The first information Doyle had concerning Reinstadt came from a Detective Stanley Holmes of the Spokane, Washington Police Department. Holmes was an Intelligence Officer who knew Doyle personally through L.E.I.U Seminars.

The information provided by Holmes reflected that Richard Reinstadt had arrived in Washington 12 to 18 months earlier and that he had been involved with the Militia in the Spokane area. Investigations concerning Reinstadt's activities in the Spokane area did not reveal criminal activity. Holmes reported that Reinstadt had relocated to the Fallbrook area of San Diego County, in California. Holmes reported that his intelligence on Reinstadt showed that he had lived in Fallbrook for several years before arriving in Spokane.

Doyle's investigative package on Reinstadt showed that Doyle next contacted Sergeant Greg Swanson, San Diego Sheriff's Department, Intelligence Bureau. Swanson, another member of L.E.I.U. told Doyle that Reinstadt was an old Klansman from long ago. He related that Reinstadt had been seen attending Aryan Nations meeting in the North Country are of San Diego. Swanson's information placed Reinstadt in close association with numerous skinheads in the San Diego area. Swanson had told Doyle that Reinstadt dropped out of sight about a year and a half or so ago. The information that Doyle shared with Swanson regarding Reinstadt's return was the first that Swanson had heard.

The package reflected Doyle's continued effort to learn every detail about Reinstadt before he would sit down with him in conversation. Doyle ran him for criminal history, automated weapons system, etc. There was even an inquiry with the FBI. Doyle reached out to his good friend, Penny Adler, but found she was out of the office. Doyle did get to talk with the Duty Agent, who did run a quick check on Reinstadt for Doyle. The FBI agent informed Doyle that Reinstadt showed an old notation regarding an affiliation with the Knights of the Ku Klux Klan.

As Sully was about to get into the actual interview portion of the file, Meg piped up. "If only Ralph had been able to talk with Penny Adler about Richard Reinstadt, instead of an Agent that had not clue about Reinstadt."

Lieutenant Flemming puzzled by Meg's observation asked, "What am I missing here? Is there something the Feds should have told Ralph about this shit head?"

Sully fielded Flemming's questions.

"I am truly sorry Lieutenant. My fault. I assume we were all up to date. Richard Reinstadt is a paid informant for the FBI."

"Ah fuck me!" Anthony Flemming yelled. He followed up with, "God damn FBI!" Sully jumped in quickly trying to cool heads with the facts.

"No! Now just settle down and listen. First of all, Agent Adler did not know about Richard Reinstadt's status with the FBI until just a few days ago. Weeks after Doyle requested the information. The sad truth of the matter is that even if she did have knowledge of Reinstadt's status with the Bureau, she would not have been allowed to divulge it to Doyle. That's just the nature of the Beast. What she would have done, I would hope, is to have gone along on the interview. Like she did with us."

After everyone had regained their composure they got back to the file and began reading Doyle's interview of Richard Reinstadt. The interview started out as guarded. It was as though Doyle was feeling Reinstadt out. Doyle's questions were, for the most part, generic. Oh, they were definitely White Supremacist related, but not directed to any particular investigation. Doyle was more or less soliciting historical type information from Reinstadt. Doyle was asking questions that he already knew the answers to. Doyle wanted to see if Reinstadt would be deceitful or not.

Doyle made notations throughout the interview report. Doyle noted after each response that Reinstadt was being truthful and at times offered up information that was new to Doyle. And, although Doyle would make a notation to verify certain aspects of Reinstadt's statements, he also noted that the data provided sounded logical.

The final questions asked by Doyle were direct. The first was about Justin Davis. Doyle told Reinstadt that Davis was a skinhead in Los Angeles and could be someone of importance in the Neo-Nazi Skinhead Movement. Reinstadt assured Sully that he had not heard of Justin Davis. But that he would ask around. The second question posed to Reinstadt was whether or not he had ever heard of a group calling itself the Guardians of Israel. Again, Reinstadt denied knowledge.

Sully asked Meg, who was holding the investigative package, if the date of the interview was listed. Meg turned the package upright to read the date which she related to Sully. Meg then thought for a moment and blurted out, "That's three days before Amanda Cavanaugh went missing!" Sully noticed notations on the back side of the Investigator's package and asked, "Meg, what did Doyle write on the back?"

Meg read, "Something about this guy does not sit right. That's the first one."

She continued, "The next one states that Reinstadt is very knowledgeable and up front with most answers. I believe him to be untruthful as to his knowledge of Justin Davis and the Guardians of Israel."

Meg then added his last note is simply, "This is a guy that needs more scrutiny."

Sully nodded his head and looked at Lieutenant Flemming and said, "Let's take a closer look at this guy, shall we?"

Flemming answered, "I'll put together a surveillance team and we'll crawl up his ass for a few weeks."

Sully agreed and told Lieutenant Flemming that the FBI would also have a surveillance team available so that twenty-four-hour coverage of Reinstadt would be an option. Sully told the group that he would leave lunch plans up to them while he went to get a clearance from Captain Morton to fax a copy of Doyle's interview to Special Agent Adler.

CHAPTER X

Doc Marten

T WAS SATURDAY MORNING. IT WAS JUST AFTER 10 A.M. when the phone rang. It was Kathy Burgess asking Sully to meet her at the Griffith Park Ranger Station. They had found another murder victim.

Kathy added, "It's another page in your Bush Fairy Killings book."

Sully told Kathy that he could meet her in about forty-five minutes or so. What Sully would learn upon arriving at the crime scene was that this latest victim was tortured and not just beaten like the others. Perhaps it was because Gregory James Jefferson was of mixed blood. Gregory had a light brown complexion with both Negro and Caucasian features.

Gregory's mother was white, while his father was African American.

Neo-Nazi Skinheads would view Gregory as a product of a Race Traitor. They would naturally take greater pleasure in doling out their brand of punishment for homosexuals, saying that queers like the victim were also of diluted Aryan blood. The differences in this attack would stand out from the murders of Gerald Grant, Richard Black and Peter Washington.

What Sully would have to learn through his investigation is what transpired before Gregory died. The events that led up to Gregory's murder, it began Friday night at 11:30 p.m. Justin Davis, along with Franklyn Andrews and Keith Thomas were cruising the Hollywood area. Justin was driving his 1988 Chevy Impala. They had just turned west on Melrose from Highland when they saw Gregory exit a gay bar. He was alone, which made him an easy target.

Gregory turned to walk down an alley next to the bar. The alley led to the parking lot at the rear of the bar. Justin drove down the alley and into the parking lot. Franklyn Andrews and Keith Thomas jumped out of the car and grabbed Gregory pulling him into the car and at the same time placing a heavy cloth hood over his head, muffling Gregory's screams.

As far as the trio of skinheads could tell, there were no witnesses in the parking lot. This, however, wasn't entirely the case. Hugh O'Brien was in the back seat of his car with his dick buried in the ass of a gay bar fly. He had just picked up Hugh O'Brien and saw Gregory get pulled into the 88 Chevy Impala. At the time he didn't think it was anything more than gay horse play.

Justin drove them through a residential neighborhood in the Los Feliz area of Los Angeles. This neighborhood wound up the hillside and abutted the Griffith Park foothills. Justin drove down a dead-end street and then up a service road to a large water tank. A car driving up to the water tank at night was most likely nothing new to the residents nearby. After all, the site was most likely very popular with young lovers. The skinheads pulled Gregory from the car and began tugging and dragging him up the trail to the top of the hill.

Justin pulled the hood off Gregory's head and greeted him.

"Hey queer boy. Which one of your parents is a fucking race traitor?"

Gregory, at the instant that Justin pulled the hood from his face, just stared at Justin in horror. You could feel the terror in Gregory's eyes. Gregory hadn't heard a word Justin uttered. He was traumatized with fear. Gregory took a deep breath and began to yell.

"Help me!"

But before he could yell another word, duct tape was placed over his mouth. Gregory was stripped of all his clothing. Leather straps were tied to his writs and ankles. He was hoisted up and suspended between two trees. It was not just 1:00 a.m.

Justin looked into Gregory's eyes. Eyes that were still filled with terror. Justin spoke softly.

"Before we can rectify your being queer and prepare you to be accepted by God as a true man, we must purify your blood. You must meet God as a black man. To do this we have to remove the Aryan blood within you that has been soiled by the mixing of the races. This Aryan blood can only be routed out of you through pain."

Gregory began to wiggle and jerk, trying to free himself. His muffled screams of panic could be heard ever so slightly through the duct tape covering his mouth. Justin grabbed hold of Gregory's right thigh while Keith Thomas took hold of his left thigh, all in an attempt to hold Gregory steady. Franklyn Andrews walked up behind Gregory so as not be seen. He didn't want Gregory to see what was in store for him.

Franklyn was holding a pair of vise grips. As he reached up and grabbed a handful of Gregory's testicles, he simultaneously secured the vise grips to his right nut. Franklyn then began to tighten the vise grips that held onto Gregory's right ball. Slowly and steadily Franklyn tightened the grip. Gregory blacked out at about the same time the testicle ruptured. The vise grip was left in place while another pair of vise grips was attached to the left nut of Gregory. Justin and Keith had let go of their hold on Gregory. There was no need now to hold him steady.

Gregory awoke to an unimaginable pain. He tried to beg for his life, but his pleas could not be heard through the tape on his mouth. Franklyn then began tightening the grip on Gregory's left testicle. Gregory again blacked out. This time well before Franklyn had tightened the grips to the point that the ball burst.

It was 2:30 a.m. when Gregory came to. The skinheads had waited for Gregory to regain consciousness before continuing to inflict pain. Justin removed the fifteen-inch swastika struck dildo from a bag. He did so with a slow deliberate action so that Gregory could see full well what was coming next. Justin squeezed a tube of Bengay on the rubber dildo and then forced it up Gregory's ass. The Bengay sent a burning sensation deep into Gregory's rectum. Gregory was then branded with the hot hermaphrodite branding iron.

The three skinheads then began beating Gregory. Several blows to the head, punches to the exposed rib cage, as well as kicks to the kneecaps. Broken ribs would puncture his right lung collapsing it. But it was steady numerous punches to the abdomen that would eventually rupture Gregory's spleen causing him to bleed internally and eventually resulting in his death which would come at 3:55 a.m. that morning. As a souvenir, Justin reached up and cut of his right ear.

As it turned out through the autopsy, all four of the "Bush Fairy" killing victims died as a result of a ruptured spleen. It was an agonizing way to leave the world behind.

The skinheads used small branches from nearby foliage to sweep away their tracks from the crime scene. They continued to sweep the trail behind them as they descended the hill back to their car.

It was 4:30 a.m. when the skinheads reached their car. As they drove down the service road and back into the neighborhood, they would almost collide with Henry Baker, who was delivering the Saturday morning Los Angeles Times. Henry Baker was used to seeing cars with young lovers emerging from the water tank road; but never expected to see three young men in the car. Baker shrugged the whole thing off. After all, this was Los Angeles! The young men could have been up behind the water tank smoking dope. Or, just three queers engaged in a homosexual ménage-a-trois.

It was 10:55 a.m. when Sully arrived at the Griffith Park Ranger Station. Kathy Burgess and Park Ranger Bill Clark were waiting inside. Seated in the lobby were two high school boys: both 17 years old. The two boys were lovers that had escaped to the hills of Griffith Park every Saturday morning. This was the only place they could be together and at the same time, keep their homosexual love affair secret.

Kathy told Sully that the two boys had found the body of Gregory Jefferson. They had told Kathy that they were out on an early morning hike when they ran across the body. What they had neglected to report to the female Detective was that they had stopped at a lower elevation on the trail and, while secluded in the bushes, gave each other a blow job. They were on their way to the top of the hill to fuck each other when they made their gruesome discovery.

After Sully was confident that the boys had given a full statement and he was satisfied that they had obtained their true identity, Sully asked them to take off their shoes. Sully grabbed a few sheets of white paper and went outside to the Bar-B-Que area. Sully placed the boys' shoes into the ash left in the pit which coated the bottoms. Sully placed the shoes on the paper making an impression of the soles. Sully would use these impressions to eliminate any tracks the two boys made at the crime scene.

Sully returned the shoes to the two boys and assured them that if they needed to contact them later that their activities in the hills of the park would not come up. The boys, although never mentioning their homosexual love making, were put at ease. Sully could read people and he could see the embarrassment and yes, even the guilt in their faces. Sully, in putting them at ease, let them know that he was not judging them.

Sully, Kathy and Ranger Clark then set out in the Ranger's 4x4 for the top of the hill. The area around the crime scene had been secured by both Park Rangers and LAPD uniformed officers. Officer Debra Hicks was keeping a log on those visiting the crime scene. Bill Clark was already on the log. He was the first Ranger on the scene. Sully and Kathy Burgess signed in on the log and the trio headed up the trail.

Upon reaching the top of the hill they could see the body of Gregory Jefferson suspended between two trees. Just as the previous victims were found. The ground in the area was free of footprints. The dirt swept clean with the exception of tennis shoe marks left by the two boys that had found Gregory. The body hung there limp and lifeless, bruised and battered. The scene was very much the same. The right ear had been severed and removed from the scene. The victim's limbs were bound with leather straps suspending him between the trees, the large dildo in his rectum. The duct tape was still over the victim's mouth and the two vise grips attached to his balls. However, these were a new addition to the modus operandi.

While Sully was examining the tape over Gregory's mouth, he noticed what appeared to be a strand of hair protruding out from under the sticky side of the tape. Hair belonging to someone other than Gregory. Kathy too was busy scouring the crime scene for evidence. And then, there it was.

"Sully!" she yelled out. "Look at this!"

It was a footprint left under the overhang of a shrub. As the two examined the print Bill Clark looked over their shoulders to get a look.

"Doc Marten." Ranger Clark stated.

"Doc Marten?" Kathy questioned.

"Yes. Doc Marten. It's the name of the boot that made that print. Look. See I am wearing a pair myself. Although that's a bit smaller than mine." Clark responded.

"They are the choice of skinheads." Interrupted Sully. "Meg was reading some of Doyle's reports and they indicated that the skinheads wear them as weapons. Their steel toes are used to literally 'put the boots' to their victim." Sully looked at Bill Clark and explained.

"Meg is my wife. She's a Reserve Officer and is helping with the investigation into the murder of Detective Ralph Doyle."

Clark nodded with understanding. Sully went on to explain how the skinheads would use white shoelaces to display their white power beliefs. Sully told them that some skinheads use red shoelaces. A throw back to the days of the "Old Warskins."

Sully had seen enough and thought it was time to get the lab crew and photo crew involved. Sully would want usual crime scene photos with special attention to the duct tape, making sure that the single strand of hair showed up. Every angle possible should be photographed, relative to the lone footprint. Sully would then instruct the lab crew to make a cast of the Doc Marten footprints. The recovery of the hair evidence for DNA was the final special instruction given by Sully. Everything else to be done by the lab was standard.

Sully, together with Kathy Burgess and Bill Clark, began to follow a small trail down the hill toward the residential neighborhood. This was the only trail that showed a continuous sweeping of the dirt. They continued on this path for about 150 yards when they came to three branches that had been torn from a large bush at the top of the hill. At this point, they found foot impressions. Three sets of Doc Marten boot prints leading up the hill to this point and three sets leading down the hill from this point. They could also detect drag marks leading up the hill to this location.

From this spot on the hill they could see the top of the water tank which was only another 200 to 300 feet down the trail. There was no way to continue down this path without destroying the foot impressions left behind by the suspects. The three returned to the top of the hill. Sully instructed both the photo and lab technicians to follow the path 150 yards until they came to the three branches and the footprints. Sully wanted photos of the branches and footprints. He wanted the lab techs to go over the branches for anything they could find. He also wanted casts made of all three-foot impressions; both left and right. Sully then instructed both crews to continue down to the water tank for more photos and forensics.

Sully, Kathy and Bill Clark then walked back down to the road where Officer Hicks was standing by with her log. Standing next to her was his good friend from the Los Angeles County Coroner's office, Bill Casey. Sully greeted Casey and made the introductions to both Kathy Burgess and Park Ranger Bill Clark. Casey had not yet responded to one of these Griffith Park Bush Fairy Killings. So, Sully filled him in on what he had missed thus far. Sully told Casey that he believed that the suspects responsible for the killings of the homosexuals in Griffith Park were also responsible for the murder of Ralph Doyle.

"I'll be on my best behavior Sully. I will leave nothing to chance with this one." Casey assured.

"I need to know your best guess on time of death." Requested Sully.

Doc. Casey requested that Sully go up the hill with him. Casey figured he could give Sully a time of death window of two hours by checking body temperature and rigor mortis. Sully returned to the body of Gregory Jefferson with Bill Casey. Casey examined the body and checked the body temp. Casey looked at Sully and said,

"Okay. Best guess, and this is just that, my best guess. I'll put the time of death between 3:00 a.m. and 5:00 a.m. Now I could be full of shit on this. But then I would have to say I'm close."

Sully was confident that they, meaning Kathy Burgess and himself had done all they could have at the crime scene. Sully had an urge to canvas the street at the end of the water tank to see if any of the residents there had seen or heard anything last night. Ranger Clark drove Sully and Kathy back down to the Ranger Station. It was now 2:45 p.m. and Sully was beyond hungry. He and Kathy used the facilities at the Ranger Station to freshen up. Outside the Ranger Station families were Bar-B-Queing. The smell of the meat sizzling over hot coals made matters worse. Sully knew that he would have to eat something before they could canvas a neighborhood.

After a quick visit to In and Out for a double-double, Sully and Kathy knocked on some doors next to the water tank. It was the last house on Maple Street, across from the access road to the water tank, where they caught a break. William Hunt, a retired camera operator from the motion pictures, had seen the skinheads' car.

Mr. Hunt, a widower, related to the Detectives that he is usually up late at night either watching an old movie or reading a good book. Hunt told them that he was closing his front drapes at about 12:30 a.m. and that is when he saw the car go up the water tank road.

"I didn't think anything of it." Hunt said. "You know these young kids go up there all the time to make love. More power to them I say."

Hunt went on to describe the car after a little prodding from Sully.

"It was an older Chevy, late eighties, I would guess. It was a large model. Impala most likely. She was dark in color. Though I couldn't really tell if it was black or dark blue. Or some other dark color. Let's see. Oh yes. It had four doors."

Sully asked Mr. Hunt if he saw any of the occupants of the car. Hunt couldn't be of any help there. He told the Detectives that the windows were tinted. Hunt was sure of this because this part of the street, which is a cul-de-sac, was very well illuminated with streetlights.

The next stop for the Detectives was the Hollywood Station. Here they would do a computer run on Gregory James Jefferson. Gregory came back negative for criminal history. He had no gun registered to him, and there were no restraining orders on record for Gregory Jefferson. When the computer searched for vehicles registered to a Gregory James Jefferson it returned with a hit on a 2004 Honda Accord, with the only address listed as Pasadena Police Department. Both Detectives got a sickening feeling. Either Gregory was a Police Officer, or he was a member of a Police Officer's family. Sully did a quick run on the name of Gregory James Jefferson for Peace Officer status, which came back negative.

Sully called the Pasadena Police Department. The phone was answered by the Desk Officer. Sully identified himself and requested the Watch Commander. Lieutenant Strickland identified himself as the Watch Commander, and Sully began his inquiry.

"Lieutenant Strickland. This is Detective Sullivan, Los Angeles Police Department Homicide."

"Yes Detective. How can I help you? Strickland questioned.

"Lieutenant, I am investigating the murder of a Gregory James Jefferson, who had a personal vehicle registered to your Department."

Lieutenant Strickland questioned with pause.

"Can you describe your victim?"

Sully responded. "He is between 21 and 26 years of age. He is a light skinned African American with both Negro and Caucasian features." Sully was interrupted by Strickland.

"I know him! He is the son of two of our Patrol Officers. They were both working today. Would you like me to arrange a meeting for you?"

Sully told Lieutenant Strickland that he and his partner would be in his office in thirty minutes. This would be the first time in his career that Sully would have to tell another Police Officer of the death of their child. Much less that the child had been murdered.

When Sully and Kathy Burgess arrived at the Pasadena Police Department Lieutenant Strickland was standing in the lobby to meet them. He had not yet called for Dwayne and Maryland Jefferson to come into the Station. Lieutenant Strickland told the Detectives that he was sorry to make them wait. He admitted that he didn't know how he could have the two officers just sitting there in his office and not reveal that their son was murdered. Sully assured the Lieutenant that he understood and that he and Kathy

Burgess did not mind waiting. Sully admitted to Strickland that he too was uncomfortable with this situation.

Dwayne and Marilyn Jefferson arrived at the Watch Commander's office. Lieutenant Strickland introduced them as Detectives William Sullivan and Kathy Burgess, Los Angeles Police Department Homicide. The two Pasadena Police Officers, unaware of what was coming, asked how they could help. Sully got that choking feeling in his throat and did all he could do to fight back the emotion.

"The hardest thing a Police Officer has to do is tell a parent that a child is dead." Sully could see it in their eyes. They knew.

"It's even more difficult to explain to them that their child was murdered. We must tell you both how very sorry we are. Your son Gregory is gone."

Sully paused. As the grieving parents tried to console each other. Dwayne was first to ask.

"How…. Can you tell us what happened?"

Sully did not want them to suffer with the morbid details. He somewhat beat around the bush in his description of Gregory's death.

"Gregory was found this morning in the hills of Griffith Park. He is the fourth victim of homicide found in the park in recent weeks."

Dwayne interrupted. "Were all the victim's gay?"

Sully now knew, at least Gregory's homosexuality was not kept secret from his parents.

"Yes." Sully answered. "All the victims were gay. The suspects in these murders are believed to be responsible for the murder of a Los Angeles Police Detective and a female informant as well."

Dwayne puzzled. Asked, "Was the Detective gay?"

"No." Responded Sully. "He was working Intelligence. He most likely hit a nerve with a group he was looking at. The very group that may be targeting homosexuals."

Sully informed Gregory's parents that the Coroner had taken possession of Gregory's body. Sully told them that he would tell the Medical Examiner to contact them. Sully and Kathy gave each of the Jefferson's a hug and again expressed their sorrow. As they turned to leave, Marilyn requested.

"Can you tell us how it happened?"

Sully looked at Kathy with a look of hesitance and then turned his attention to the parents.

"Because this is an ongoing investigation involving no less than six victims, we cannot get into details. I say this as the Chief Detective, as a fellow Police Officer and a parent, I tell you don't ask about the death. Remember his life and the joys he brought you."

Dwayne nodded as he held his wife as if to thank Sully for not revealing the ugly details of their son's murder.

Sully and Kathy left the Pasadena Police Station. As they headed back to the Hollywood Station where Kathy had left her car, Sully turned his head toward her and stated.

"Remind me Monday to take the title 'Bush Fairy Killings' off the Homicide book and replace it with the 'Gregory James Jefferson, et al Murders.'"

Kathy looked at Sully and agreed.

"Good call Sully."

Before calling it a day, the Detectives would put out a want on Gregory's car. The want would be entered into the California Law Enforcement telecommunications system. Anyone running Gregory's vehicle license number in this system would be alerted to the fact that the vehicle was wanted in relation to a homicide investigation and to alert Detectives Sullivan and Burgess at the Robbery Homicide Division. What neither Sully nor Kathy realized was that at 2:00 a.m. Sunday morning they would be awakened from a deep sleep.

Kurt Roth was the bartender at Brent's Tavern on Melrose. Friday night, after closing, which actually made it 2:00 a.m. Saturday, Kurt saw Gregory's car still in the parking lot. He really didn't think much of it, believing perhaps that Gregory had hooked up with someone. Kurt noted that the car was still parked there Saturday afternoon when he came back to reopen the Tavern. Kurt closed the bar at 1:00 a.m. Sunday morning. It was just about 1:30 a.m. when he went to the parking lot and saw that Gregory's car was still parked there. Kurt knew Gregory pretty well as Gregory was a regular at the Tavern. This was not like Gregory to abandon his car for a couple of days. Kurt called the Hollywood Station to report his friend missing, and at the same time reported his vehicle abandoned. The Desk Officer ran the vehicle license and read the Homicide want.

When Sully got the phone call at 2:00 a.m., he asked the Desk Officer to send a unit to Brent's Tavern and impound the vehicle. He requested that Kurt drive himself to the Police Station and await the arrival of himself and Detective Burgess.

The interview with Kurt Roth was relatively quick. Kurt told the Detectives that he had last seen Gregory Friday night. He had been at the Tavern and had a few drinks. Gregory did have conversations with other patrons in the Bar but left alone. Kurt recalled that Gregory left shortly after 11:00 p.m. He told the Detectives that he closed up at 1:00 a.m. He observed that when he left, Gregory's car was still parked in the lot, as were a couple of other cars. Kurt remarked that sometimes guys hook up inside the Bar and then go out and get it on in their cars.

Kurt related that when he arrived at Brent's Tavern Saturday afternoon, he noticed that Gregory's car was still parked in the same spot. He added that he didn't become concerned until he closed up Saturday night and found Gregory's car was still parked in the lot.

"It was Sunday morning at 1:00 a.m. when I closed the Bar." Kurt corrected his statement to Sully.

Sully acknowledged the correction.

"I knew what you meant. Let me ask you this. You said guys usually hook up inside the Bar and then go out to the parking lot and get it on in their cars. Is that correct?"

"Yes," answered Kurt.

"Do you think you could ask around with your regulars and see if anyone was getting it on when Gregory was abducted? See if anyone saw something unusual?" Sully asked.

"Yes Sir. I'll start asking when I open this afternoon." Kurt responded.

"Good." Sully stated as he handed Kurt his card. "My cell number is on there. Call me when you located someone who can shed some light on things. Okay?"

"Yes Sir, Detective. I'll help in anyway I can." Kurt assured.

CHAPTER XI

HUNT FOR THE DILDO

I T WAS MONDAY MORNING AND BOTH SULLY AND KATHY Burgess were at Hollywood Division to address the Day Watch Roll Call. They were armed with photographs of the fifteen-inch swastika dildo. The intent was to let the Patrol Officers check out the sex shops in their respective beats and see if anyone knew where they came from. Sully had first thought about tasking Meg with this job, but then, thought better of it. He didn't want her coming out of the sex toy shops wondering if dicks really came in such large sizes and then coming home and sizing him up.

At any rate, having the Beat Officers check out their known sex shops would be quicker. The Watch Commander called roll and gave out the unit assignments. After which he turned the troops over to Sully.

Sully knew how roll call could get. Most cops had no self control when it came to humor. And, asking these guys to go out and find you a fifteen-inch rubber cock had laughter written all over it. But as Sully stood in front of the officers, he observed that half of the room was made up of female officers. No sweat, he thought. These guys are not going to make rude sexual jokes in front of their female partners.

"I'm Detective Sullivan and this is my partner, Detective Burgess of Robbery Homicide." Sully began.

"Now I want to pass out some pictures. Sorry ladies, I know this isn't what you signed on for. What we need you to do is canvas your sex shops and see if any of the clerks can identify it."

Then it began. One cop in the rear of the room yelled out, "Don't need to check with a clerk. I can identify it. It's a big dick!" And the room roared with laughter.

A female officer raised her hand, as if she were in a classroom. Poised and innocently she asked, "Detective, if we find it, do we get to try it out?"

Sully waited for the laughter to die down and continued.

"I am glad that I could come here today and bring you something that would bring a smile to your face. For some of you," as he looked at the young female officer, "Perhaps a daily smile." Sully got a laugh of his own and then continued on a more serious side.

"This dildo is unique in that there is a swastika molded into the head of the penis. Thus far, we have four homicides where one of these dildos was left in the rectum of the victim. All of the victims were young, gay men. The last victim was the son of two Pasadena Police Officers. In addition, the suspects responsible for these murders are suspected in the murder of an LAPD Detective who was, we believe, getting close to arresting them. So, by all means have fun with this sexy little task. But please, at the same time know that you are doing a serious job."

With this, the officers set out to do their jobs. Sully figured if the swastika dildos were out there in circulation, then guys would find them. As for Meg, Sully thought he would give her the responsibility of finding Robin Peterson. Sully had the idea that when Miss Peterson was confronted by a mother figure like Meg, and then added Anthony Flemming, an older Black man who exudes authority to the mix... Well maybe, just maybe Miss Peterson would cooperate.

Sully knew that Lieutenant Flemming was itching to get all over Richard Reinstadt. Sully, however, believed Reinstadt for the moment was the FBI's problem. Although Sully felt in his gut that Reinstadt was in some way connected to the murder of his friend, Doyle, he knew full well that the strongest leads to date were with the Gregory Jefferson murder. Sully believed that once they made an arrest in the Griffith Park murders, things would fall into place.

Sully would shape his thoughts at the 2:00 p.m. briefing that Captain Morton had arranged. As Sully and Kathy Burgess where leaving the Hollywood Station, they passed by the front desk. Just as a guy walked in with a bundle of morning papers from the Los Angeles Times an idea hit Sully. Just like in the cartoons when the light bulb in the head comes on. Sully grabbed Kathy's arm and stopped her in her tracks. Sully then asked the young man with the papers if he had a phone number for the person at the Times responsible for dispatching route drivers. The young man gave Sully the number and left to continue his deliveries.

Sully called the LA Times dispatch and was greeted by Harold Grimes. Grimes was sixty-five years old and had begun his career at the Los Angeles Times when he was eighteen. For the past twenty-five years Grimes coordinated the home delivery routes. Sully identified himself and explained that there was an outside chance that the person delivering the morning paper, on Maple Street in the Los Feliz area, may have seen the suspects driving away from a homicide.

Grimes checked his route roster and located the name of Henry Baker, who Grimes reported had been delivering on that route for the past five years. Grimes furnished a cell phone number for Baker. Sully called the number which was in fact answered by Henry Baker. Henry explained that he had just completed his deliveries and was headed back to the LA Times office at Fountain and Vine. Sully told Mr. Baker that he would meet him there at his office.

"I know you must be tired and anxious to get home, but I just need a minute of your time."

"You got it Detective, I'm only too glad to help you guys out." Baker responded.

Sully and Kathy met with Henry Baker at the LA Times office. It really was nothing more than a large one room store front where the delivery folks could put their papers together and wrap them in plastic, protecting them from the elements. The Detectives explained that they were investigating a murder that took place at about 3:00 a.m. or so on Saturday morning. Sully told Baker that the suspects had parked their vehicle behind the water tank at the end of Maple Street.

"Oh Yeah. Sure. Yeah, I was up there delivering papers. I saw the car. I'm sure of it." Baker responded.

Sully interjected, "What time was that?"

Baker answered, "It was just past 4:30 a.m. They almost hit me when they came down the road onto Maple Street."

"They?" Questioned Sully.

"Yeah. There were three of them in the car. All guys. They appeared to have shaved heads. I figured they were up there queering off or smoking dope is all." Baker accounted.

Sully asked Baker if he got a good look at the suspects' vehicle. Baker told Sully that they were driving an older 1980's vintage Chevy Impala. Baker described the car as a four-door black sedan. The color was not clean or very well taken care of. Baker then added. "Oh yeah. The windshield has a long crack. Just a single line crack about 16 inches down; going across the front of the driver's face."

Henry Baker didn't recall license plates or any other identifying characteristics about the car. In all fairness, he had only gotten a brief glimpse at the suspects. The fact that he was able to tell that there were three Caucasians with shaved heads, was significant enough.

Sully and Kathy Burgess were done with Henry Baker for the moment and were about to head downtown when Sully's cell phone rang. It was Kurt Roth from Brent's Tavern.

"Detective Sullivan. Kurt here. I have someone here that may have seen Gregory being pulled into a car."

Sully assured Kurt that they were on their way and could be there in ten minutes. Kurt told Sully not to rush that he and Hugh O'Brien would await their arrival. It was almost ten minutes to the second when Sully and Kathy entered Brent's Tavern. Kurt greeted the Detectives like they were lifelong friends. Sully thought this must be a gay thing. All this warm and fuzzy reception like they were displaced relatives.

Kurt introduced Hugh O'Brien to the Detectives. After the round of handshakes, the four sat down at a table. Sully got right to the point. He laid a photo of Gregory on the table.

"Do you know this person?"

"I saw him here in the Bar Friday night. We didn't talk. I was kinda occupied with some other guy at the Bar. They call him Bar

Fly. I mean I noticed him for sure. The guy was cute. But I had already hooked up with, you know, the Bar Fly dude. Well, I saw this guy," O'Brien now pointing to the picture of Gregory Jefferson, "again in the parking lot. I had just mounted the Bar Fly in the back seat of my car. Your guy was walking into the parking lot from the alley when this black 1988 Chevy Impala pulled up along side of him. Two guys with shaved heads got out and then pulled him into their car. I just thought that they were clowning around."

"Anything else about the car?" Sully questioned.

"Yes. When they drove through the lot, in order to turn around, I saw the bumper sticker. It was… Well… I don't know what it was exactly. I mean. I know exactly what it was. I just don't know what it means."

"Okay." Sully interrupted. "What did it say?"

"RaHoWa. Capital 'R' - small 'a' - capital 'H'- small 'o' - capital 'W' - small 'a'," explained O'Brien.

Sully thought to himself. I'll never understand these dickhead skinheads. Sully would learn later from Special Agent Adler that RaHoWa stands for "Racial Holy War."

Sully asked O'Brien. "Are you sure about the car?"

O'Brien smiled, "I had a 1988 Chevy Impala when I was in high school. The car I know."

Sully left Brent's Tavern feeling confident that he was making headway in the investigation. He turned to Kathy as they hit the sidewalk outside the Bar.

"What do you think Kathy? Do you feel as I do that we have made some headway today?"

Kathy responded. "Yes. I feel pretty good about what we have accomplished today. What with the information we received from Baker from the LA Times and O'Brien from the gay bar, I think we are really on to something here."

It was now 1:00 p.m. and Sully and Kathy were no closer to downtown L.A. where at 2:30 p.m. they would have to brief Captain Morton and a select few on the investigation thus far. Sully knew too that Captain Morton was going to ask for a plan of attack. Sully hadn't given any thought to an investigative strategy yet. It really wasn't his cup of tea. Sully was a Detective. He went where the case took him. He wasn't all wrapped up in administrative crap like operational plans.

Sully's phone again rang, and he answered it with the same non-descript professional, but yet impersonal, Department approved style.

"Detective Sullivan. Los Angeles Police Department. May I help you?"

"Sure, you can big boy!" The young sexy female voice answered.

"I just hope you're man enough, because the dick I have in my hand would put most men to shame." She continued.

"Who is this?" Sully asked.

"Detective, this is Officer Sanchez. Vickie Sanchez. I have found your swastika rubber dicky!" She informed.

"We are at a sex shop at Western and Santa Monica. The clerk here is very helpful and can't wait to talk to you."

Sully turned to Kathy and told her that one of the Hollywood units located a sex shop that dealt in big swastika cocks. Western and Santa Monica was only about ten minutes from their location at Brent's Tavern, given that traffic wasn't fucked up.

As Sully and Kathy pulled to the curb on Santa Monica at Western, they noted that the name of the sex shop was Danny's Peep Show. The establishment was full service. They had all the latest adult toys. Anything you wanted from bondage through heterosexual and into homosexual. If you wanted to cram it, or be crammed, you could find what you wanted at this Love Palace. Besides the toys there were magazines and movies in VHS or DVD. The movie selection satisfied any urge imaginable. And then, of course, there were the viewing booths. Here a visitor could pay a token to view a portion of a film. The film of their choice. They could continue to purchase the viewing rights for a few minutes at a time. The booths were generally known to be coated with cum.

Officer Sanchez greeted Sully and Kathy. She was holding a fifteen-inch dildo with a swastika molded into the penis head. It was the same female officer that had made jokes in roll call. Sully couldn't resist.

"Whoa! That's a good grip you have there on that man thing officer!"

Officer Sanchez laughed. "Yeah. I had that coming. No pun on the 'coming' Detective."

Sully laughed and told Vickie Sanchez that she was quick with her humor and if it weren't for the time restraints, he would enjoy bantering back and forth with her. Vickie told Sully and Kathy that the proprietor was Earl Dicks.

"No kidding Detectives. This guy's name is actually 'Dicks.'" Vickie related.

Dicks, according to Vickie, had sold several of the big swastika engraved dildos over the past several months.

Vickie led the Detectives into the store and introduced them to Earl Dicks. Sully introduced himself and Kathy to Earl. Earl was in his mid-forties and about 6 foot in height. He weighed all of about 140 lbs. soaking wet. This is the guy you would expect to see pictured next to the word string bean in Webster's Dictionary. Earl was the closest thing you could come to being an Oakie and still have all your teeth.

Earl told the Detectives that he had sold several of the swastika dildos to some skinheads that come into the store from time to time. Earl told the Detectives that the last dildo that he sold was to three skinheads last Friday night around 9:00 p.m. Sully asked Earl if he thought he could describe the three.

"Ah. Yah know I'm not real good with picturing folk." Earl said. "But we do have security cameras here. They would have to be on our tapes. I could get them for you if you would like me to."

Sully acknowledged Earl's desire to help.

"Please Earl, if you could give us the tapes for Friday night that would be great. I'll tell you what I'll do Earl. I'll make copies and return them to you. Would that be Okay?"

"Well, yah Detective. That'd be just fine."

Sully and Kathy gave Earl a receipt for the security tapes. They gave a big thank you and a job well done to Vicky Sanchez and her partner. As they turned to walk away Sully realized that Vickie was still standing on the sidewalk holding the hulk size cock.

"Vickie, are you going to return that to Earl?" Sully asked.

Vickie grinned, held up the dildo and responded.

"Maybe. Maybe not."

Now they were pushing the limit on time. Sully wanted to get the video tapes to the photo lab before their briefing with Captain Morton. Sully was hoping that he could get a copy made to run through at the briefing while the lab duplicated some stills of the skinheads purchasing the big rubber dick.

It was just after 2:00 o'clock when they dropped off the video and gave the photo technician instructions. Thankfully, the briefing was being held in the Chief's conference room at Parker Center.

CHAPTER XII

THE BRIEFING

ULLY AND KATHY ENTERED THE CAPTAIN'S
conference room. It was 2:23 p.m. and the room had already
begun to fill. Lieutenant Flemming and Meg were a welcome
sight. Sully didn't know most of the people in the room. Kathy then
pointed out the Captain. Stephanie Porter was across the room.
Then Meg nudged Sully and pointed to Penny Adler who had just
arrived. Sully thought, and then began bitching just a little.

"You know, I wish that Captain Morton would have asked me
about this. I am not adequately prepared for this briefing. I don't
even know why all these stuffed shirts are here."

About then Captain Morton entered the room with the Chief.
The Captain was a no-nonsense guy and got right down to business.
He basically laid out the murder of Ralph Doyle and his skinhead
informant, Amanda Cavanaugh. With that he was done. Well, with
the exception of putting it all on Sully.

Sully stood and thanked Captain Morgan for his introduction.
Sully then addressed the group.

"I am at a bit of a disadvantage here and I want to apologize in
advance if I offend any of you. Before we get started, I would like to
go around the room and get each one of you to introduce yourselves
to the rest of the group. I would also like you to explain exactly why
your presence is needed here today."

Before Sully could point to any one person and say let's start with you, Captain Morton stood up and interrupted.

"Hold that thought for one minute folks. Just excuse us for a minute."

Captain Morton marched Sully out of the room followed by the Chief. Captain Stephanie Porter joined them. She thought Sully might need an ally.

"What are you doing Detective Sullivan?" Morton began.

"Captain, I am protecting my investigation. I don't know these people and what's more I don't know that they need to know about the investigation at this time." Sully replied.

Morton interrupted again. "This investigation is about the murder of one of our own!"

It was Sully's turn to interrupt. "No Sir. It's more than that. The only reason that you are in the dark is because Kathy Burgess and I have been busting our asses since the Friday murder of Gregory Jefferson. We have been running leads all day. I can tell you we have one hell of a briefing to give. But I am not giving up my investigation to a room full of people I don't know!"

Captain Porter jumped in, "I think we should excuse those that are not needed and get to the progress of Sullivan's and Burgess's investigation. Let's see where they want to take this. Shall we?"

They re-entered the room and Sully called out to Lieutenant Flemming, Meg, of course, and Special Agent Penny Adler. Sully apologized to the others for taking up their time and excused them.

The Chief looked around and remarked.

"Let's take this into my office. It's smaller and more personable."

Sully began by explaining that it was apparent that Doyle was murdered as a direct result of his work on a specific white power group by the name of "the Guardians of Israel." He added that someone in the movement was able to detect Doyle's investigation and apparently identify Amanda Cavanaugh as Doyle's informant. Sully explained that at this point they believe that Richard Reinstadt may be the individual who ordered the murders of Doyle and Cavanaugh.

Sully then explained that they have now connected four additional homicides to Doyle's murder. Sully advised that the latest homicide involved Gregory Jefferson. Sully described Jefferson as a young male homosexual whose mother was white and father black. Sully related that the suspects in this murder are three Neo-Nazi Skinheads.

"We have a vehicle description for the suspects. A vehicle that we should have no trouble locating. About an hour ago we dropped a security tape at the photo lab. We are confident that this tape will provide us with photographs of the suspects."

"There are some, who will protect our avenue of investigation. They will claim that the murder of a cop takes priority over the killing of a few fags. I will tell you now that I expect those of you in this room to back us up on our choices. I'm telling you that the road to solving Doyle's murder is through the arrests of the skinheads responsible for the murder of Gregory Jefferson. Oh, and Gregory's parents - they are both Pasadena Police Officers. They are both relying on our Department to solve their son's murder."

Captain Morton told Sully that he was sorry for creating a circus-like atmosphere earlier. He told Sully to go with his gut and he would stay out of the way. He also assured Sully that he would be close by to give aid where needed. Sully nodded and the two shook hands.

Sully again took charge.

"Okay. Here is what I have in mind. First, Lieutenant Flemming. You and your surveillance team will stand down."

Sully could see Flemming about to interrupt in protest. Sully put his hand up.

"Don't. You and Meg are going to team up and locate the sixteen-year-old female skinhead that Doyle had talked to Meg about. Robin Peterson, I think it was."

Meg told Sully he was correct. It was Robin Peterson.

"Penny Adler and the FBI." Sully began again, "Your people will conduct surveillance of Reinstadt. But I don't want to burn him. So, let's try working a week of Monday, Wednesday and Friday and then a week of working Tuesday, Thursday and Saturday. We'll analyze what we get after the two weeks."

Penny agreed with Sully's plan with regards to Reinstadt. Sully continued.

"Kathy and I will continue to follow up on the leads we developed in the Gregory Jefferson matter."

Just then the photo lab technician arrived at the Chief's office to let them know that they had completed duplicating the security tapes from Danny's Peep Show sex shop. The time was indicated in the corner of the tape. Sully ran the tape up to 8:30 p.m. Earl Dick's had reported that the skinheads entered at about 9:00 p.m. Sully figured they could view the tape on scan until they detected the skinheads. This particular tape came from the camera behind the clerk. It would afford the best view of the individuals standing at the counter making purchases.

The tape first depicted a skinhead in the background of the sex shop at 8:57 p.m. This individual would later be identified as Keith Thomas. A couple of minutes later and the camera would record the presence of two additional skinheads. They too would eventually be identified as Justin Davis and Franklyn Andrews.

At 9:10 p.m. all three skinheads stood in front of the clerk. Their purchase of a fifteen-inch dildo would be recorded. The only problem with the tape was that it did not show a swastika on the head of the giant rubber penis. Sully thought that the lab would enlarge portions of the penis caught on tape and see if they could see a swastika molded into the dildo.

The photo lab technician told the group seated in the Chief's office that the photo lab would have still photos of the three skinheads very shortly. Sully assigned the task of picking up those photos to Meg and Lieutenant Flemming.

Sully instructed.

"The two of you can pick up the photographs when we are done here. When you locate and interview Robin Peterson, see if she will put some names to the photos."

Meg responded, "We'll get the photos. We can possibly show them to Peterson by the end of the day."

Sully looked puzzled and questioned.

"Are you sure?"

Meg answered, "Yes. Well pretty sure anyway. Doyle's file has Robin Peterson living at home with her parents. We can stop by there just before dinner. Maybe we'll get lucky."

Lieutenant Flemming added, "If Peterson gives us the names to go along with these photos, then we could go back into the files and see if Doyle has an address for these three as well."

Sully agreed that Meg and the Lieutenant should attempt to interview Robin Peterson today if possible.

Sully added. "If Peterson identifies these three and one of them turns out to be Justin Davis, then Doyle may have an address to go with him. Then Lieutenant, you can put your surveillance team on him. Especially if he is driving a 1988 Chevy 4 door Impala, dark in color. In fact, if any of the persons identified by Peterson is driving this car, then that's the guy we want to keep tabs on."

Flemming agreed. As did Meg. But then Special Agent Adler had a thought.

"Sully," she said. "Your surveillance team leader should coordinate with our team leader. If Reinstadt is behind the Guardians of Israel, well, we wouldn't want our surveillance teams tripping over each other should your suspect and Reinstadt hook up."

Sully thanked Penny. This was a good point. The two teams should have the intelligence data on each other's targets. Their movements should be reported to the other team's leader, so as to avoid the two teams coming together without some type of coordination. Sully knew that Agent Adler would have her team on Reinstadt first thing Wednesday morning. He felt too that the earliest Flemming's team could be in place was Wednesday morning as well. That is, if they located Peterson and she identified the suspects and they were able to locate either the Chevy or the group's leader, Justin Davis.

You know that sometimes in police work you just get lucky. As it turned out, Meg and Lieutenant Anthony Flemming were able to locate Robin Peterson. She lived at home with her parents. They were middle class Americans with careers. Robin's mother, Judy, was a Dental Assistant and her father, Frederick, was a tool and die man employed in a small machine shop. The Peterson's were ideal parents. Both now in their late forties, they were much in tune to their daughter's activities. When the two police officers, Lieutenant Flemming and Meg Sullivan showed up on their doorstep, they knew that they wanted to talk to Robin regarding her involvement with the skinheads.

The Petersons had discovered the white supremacist literature in her room. From there they did what most parents would be afraid to do. They basically searched her room and everything and anything in it. The Petersons found notes and messages that related to skinhead activities. They found the names of other kids that they knew nothing about.

Meg figured that Frederick and Judy Peterson must have uncovered Robins' involvement in the Guardians of Israel early and nipped it in the bud before Robin got too involved. The Petersons invited their two guests into the dining room and had them take a seat. Mr. Peterson went into the den and retrieved a box and placed it on the table in front of them.

"I suppose you'll be wanting this crap!" He stated.

Meg and Anthony Flemming began to sift through the box of notes, messages, literature and yes, even photographs of Robin Peterson, taken with several skinheads, both male and female. As luck would have it, there was Robin Peterson pictured with all three of the skinheads that showed up on the security tapes at Danny's Peep Show.

"Does this help you officers?" Asked Judy Peterson.

"Yes. This is very interesting stuff." Answered Meg.

"But we would really like to ask your daughter some questions. That is, if you don't mind."

Frederick Peterson responded to Meg's inquiry.

"Let's be honest here Okay? I mean, we are law abiding people and we want to help you folks. Believe me we want to help you do your job. But you must understand as parents we are duty bound to protect our daughter. We have protected her from the influence of those Nazi bastards that tried to lure her into their evil world. Now we want to know the truth. Does she need a lawyer? Do we need to protect her from you?"

Meg thought she could relate Mother-to-Mother to Judy Peterson. But it was Anthony Flemming that took the lead.

"I can appreciate your concern for your daughter. You have protected her from evil influence and now want to be sure you don't turn around and throw her to the wolves, so to speak. I can assure you of this Mr. and Mrs. Peterson, we have no reason to suspect that your daughter Robin is involved in any criminal activity. Our reason for being here is to ask her about certain members of the Guardians of Israel who we do believe are involved in criminal activity. We believe your daughter can assist us in identifying these individuals. I will promise you this much. If, while talking to Robin, she gives me any indication that she has participated in any of the criminal activity which we have an interest in, well, Mr. and Mrs. Peterson, I will stop her and instruct you to call a lawyer. Is that fair enough?"

The Petersons agreed and they summoned their daughter, Robin, out from her room.

Robin, it turned out, was the furthest thing from a white supremacist. How she got mixed up with the likes of the Guardians of Israel was a bewilderment of its own. Robin, as it turned out, did hang out with the skinheads for about ten weeks before her parents interceded.

As it turned out, Robin Peterson was extremely intelligent. She had what you might call a photographic memory. Her ties to the Guardians of Israel were more through curiosity rather than true interest. Robin's explanation to Flemming and Meg Sullivan for her infatuation with the group was very believable. The more Robin talked about the group, the more apparent it was becoming that Robin was not involved in any of the group's criminality.

After Meg and Anthony Flemming were sure that they were not going to get to a place that would place Robin in legal peril, they showed her the pictures of the three skinheads purchasing the dildo at Danny's Peep Show sex shop. Robin identified the three as Justin Davis; Keith Thomas; and Franklyn Andrews. Robin told them that Justin Davis was the leader of the group and that the others just followed along and did whatever he told them to do.

Robin described Justin Davis as a "sicko." She told the investigators that he got off on watching others suffer. She told them that a fourteen-year-old girl, by the name of Kelly Anderson, wanted to join the Guardians. Justin told her that she would have to fuck four skinheads of his choice. When Kelly protested, claiming she was a virgin, Justin laughed and told her he would watch her cherry being ruptured with great pain. Robin told them that Kelly ran off in tears. Robin stated.

"You know, Justin just wanted to see her suffer as she had her cherry popped."

Meg asked, "What kind of car does Justin drive?"

"It's an older black Chevy. A big car with four doors." She answered.

CHAPTER XIII

SPECIAL DELIVERY

MONDAY WOULD COME TO AN END PROVING TO BE A very productive day in the investigation into a series of murders believed to be the responsibility of the Guardians of Israel. Sully and Kathy Burgess would uncover conclusive evidence that Jefferson and other homosexuals were the victims of hate. This was the hate of Neo-Nazi's bent on eliminating homosexuals all together.

The identities of three of these skinheads would be learned through the combined efforts of William Sullivan and Kathy Burgess, as well as, Meg Sullivan and Anthony Flemming. They would now, at least know those responsible for the murder of Gregory Jefferson and very possibly the other three Griffith Park victims: Gerald Clark, Richard Black and Peter Washington. Sully was just as confident that Justin Davis was present during the murder of his good friend, Ralph Doyle. Justin also was most likely in Bakersfield for the murder of Amanda Cavanaugh.

Now there came the task of proving all of this theory and conjuncture. One would have to admit that it all looked promising on paper. But it was solid evidence that was needed for convictions. Sully was now on edge. He would be the first to admit that he was anxious. He only wished that it were now Wednesday night and not just Monday night. After all, if it had been Wednesday night, they could sit down and analyze the day's activities and movements of both Justin Davis and, what's more, Richard Reinstadt.

As it would turn out not being set up on Richard Reinstadt would prove to be an error. Apparently Sully hit a nerve when he interviewed Reinstadt. At the very least Richard Reinstadt must have felt threatened more by Sully and the interview than he did with Penny Adler and Kathy Burgess.

Reinstadt left his Fallbrook home at 1:00 a.m. Tuesday morning. He arrived in Los Angeles, more specific two doors down the street from the Sullivan house at 2:15 a.m. Reinstadt sat in his car until 3:00 a.m. waiting and observing the neighborhood. Reinstadt wanted to be sure that everyone was fast asleep. He wanted to be sure that his actions at the Sullivan household would not be detected.

As it turned out before leaving his home in Fallbrook, Reinstadt had constructed a device for murder. It was a 12-inch pipe bomb constructed of a two-inch nipple and end gaps. The bomb was filled with smokeless black powder. A hole had been drilled into the end cap allowing the electrical wires to pass through and connect to a flash bulb contained inside, amidst the gunpowder. The wires which were attached to a nine-volt battery were connected to a mercury switch. A switch commonly found in a thermostat. The mercury would remain at one end of the tube so long as the safety rod was in place. Once the safety rod was removed the device was armed. To activate the device, one would need to move the explosive device causing the mercury to flow to the opposite end of the tube. This would complete the electrical connection, setting off the flashbulb which would cause the gunpowder to burn, exploding the pipe. Taped to the pipe with duct tape was a glass jar filled with carpet tacks.

Reinstadt placed the explosive device in front of the front screen door at the Sullivan home. Reinstadt then removed the safety rod arming the pipe bomb. Reinstadt was back home and in his bed in Fallbrook by 5:00 a.m. It would be 5:30 when Sully and Meg would wake up to the alarm clock and ready themselves for work. The one thing that Reinstadt could not know was that neither Sully nor Meg hardly ever entered or departed their home through the front door. Normally they came and went through the rear of the house.

On this Tuesday morning, Sully, Meg, Anthony Flemming and Kathy Burgess all reported to Major Crimes Division. Their day would be devoted to Doyle's files and all he had on Justin Davis, Keith Thomas, and Franklyn Andrews. It was twelve noon when the group of hardworking investigators decided to grab lunch. Baja Fresh would be the selection of the day. While enjoying lunch they had no way of knowing the events that were unfolding at the Sullivan home.

It was 12:15 in the afternoon when the mail truck parked in front of the Sullivan's home at 12420 Haiterous Place. Michael Sanders, the Postal Carrier, had a large envelope size 11-inch x 14-inch. It was a portrait size envelope addressed to Harold Parks of 12420 Haiterous Place. The fact of the matter was however, that Harold Parks resided at 14220 Haiterous Place. Somebody had transposed the street numbers when addressing the package.

Postman Sanders walked onto the Sullivan's front porch. As he stood in front of the front door, he saw a box fifteen-inches long and six-inches wide. The box was wrapped in brown shipping paper. The postman didn't see any address markings on the box but shrugged it off. Sanders believed that the package was delivered by either FEDEX or UPS and laid down in front of the door upside down. Sanders rang the doorbell to the Sullivan home, but he did not get an answer. Sanders decided he would place his large envelope between the screen door and the front door of the residence.

Sanders reached down to move the box out of the way so that he could open the screen door. As Sanders moved the box, the mercury within the thermostat switch rolled down the glass tube and completed the electrical connection. The bulb flashed in the powder in a matter of one hundredth of a second and the pipe bomb exploded with such force that it blew out the front door of the Sullivan home. The windows on either side of the door were shattered. The body of Postal Carrier Michael Sanders was thrown forty feet out onto the Sullivan's front yard. His body was torn apart by fragments of the pipe, as well as hundreds of carpet tacks.

Sullivan's neighbor, Jon Quon heard the explosion and ran out of his home, directly across the street from the Sullivan's. Mr. Quon was shocked when he saw the horror across the street at the

Sullivan's. The air was still filled with dirt, debris, and smoke. Jon Quon saw the torn and bloodied body on the Sullivan lawn. Mr. Quon had no way of knowing that the body was that of a Postal Worker. The clothing worn by the victim was so badly burned one could in no way tell it was the uniform of a mailman. Quon probably didn't even hear the 911 operator as he just continued to yell, "send them to 12420 Haiterous Place!"

The Fire Department and paramedics arrived first. It was quite obvious that Michael Sanders was dead. The body was covered with a yellow tarp. When the first police unit arrived, the paramedics identified themselves for the police incident log. They wrote out a response ticket explaining their actions at the scene. Actually, their intrusion into the crime scene was minimal. Before clearing from the call, the paramedics told the officer that the neighbor across the street, Mr. Quon, was the reporting party.

Officer Rivera questioned Mr. Quon.

"Sir. Can you tell me what happened here?"

Mr. Quon responded, "I hear big noise. I run out a see Detective Sullivan home blown up!"

The officer questioned, "What do you mean Detective?"

Mr. Quon attempted to clarify his response.

"Detective Sullivan is living there. He is L.A.P.D. Murder Detective."

Officer Rivera had no way of knowing that the dead man on the front lawn was indeed Postal Carrier Michael Sanders. The mail truck parked on the street hadn't yet made an impression on anyone. Rivera called in that he had a possible officer down at his location citing that the victim officer might be a Detective Sullivan, LAPD. He requested that Robbery Homicide respond. Officer Rivera was not one hundred percent sure that the dead man was a cop. But he was in fact one hundred percent sure that the damage caused to the front of the residence at 12420 Haiterous Place was the result of an improvised explosive device. Officer Rivera requested that the Bomb Squad respond to the crime scene as well.

Captain Stephanie Porter was notified by Communications Division that a homicide by bombing had occurred at 12420 Haiterous Place. She was told that the victim may be the homeowner, an LAPD Detective known only as Sullivan, at this time. Captain Porter knew full well that Sully was with Detective Kathy Burgess at Major Crimes Division reviewing Ralph Doyle's files.

Captain Porter dispatched a team of Detectives to the Sullivan home. Then she telephoned Kathy Burgess's cell phone.

"Hello. This is Kathy," she answered.

"Detective Burgess, this is Captain Porter. Is Detective Sullivan with you? She questioned.

"Yes. He is right here. We are having lunch." Burgess responded.

"Good. That's good. Is his wife there too?" She continued.

"Yes. She is here also. So is Lieutenant Flemming. Why? What's up?" Kathy Burgess could sense something was wrong.

Captain Porter, in a very cool and collected manner, began to fill Burgess in on what she knew regarding the bombing at Sullivan's home. The Captain suggested that all four of them respond to the crime scene and see if they could be of assistance to the team she assigned.

Porter was sure to caution. "You guys are to offer assistance through your insight. Don't get in the way or interfere. Do you understand what I am saying?" Porter asked.

Burgess assured Captain Porter that they would stay in the background. By the time the four arrived at the Sullivan home the Detectives had established that the dead man was the Postal Carrier, Michael Sanders. Sully, Meg, and Anthony Flemming stood across the street and out of the way. Kathy Burgess walked over to talk to her co-workers from Robbery Homicide Division. She told them that Captain Porter had asked that they standby here in case they could be of assistance. She added that they were told to stay of the way.

Jody Feder was the lone Bomb Technician on the scene. The area had been cleared of any secondary devices. The other Bomb Techs that had responded with Officer Feder were called away to investigate a suspicious package at Los Angeles International Airport. Jody was more than capable of processing this crime scene by herself. She had not been with the LAPD all that long. She had only six years on the job. Bomb Technicians are normally more seasoned officers. Jody, however, had served four years in the

United States Army before joining the LAPD. In the Army she was assigned to the Ordinance Unit. Jody had three years of experience defusing explosives for the Army. The LAPD was fortunate in getting her.

Feder had been processing the crime scene for nearly forty-five minutes and had been able to recover dozens of pipe fragments, a section of a nine-volt battery, the metal tip of a flashbulb and a small puddle of mercury. There would be more bomb fragments recovered from the body of the Postal Carrier. Feder was assisted in her sweep of the crime scene by Detectives from the Criminal Conspiracy Section, C.C.S. It would be the responsibility of CCS to investigate the bombing at the Sullivan home. It would take Jody Feder less than eight hours to reconstruct the explosive device placed on the front porch of the Sullivan home.

Sully, Meg, Kathy Burgess and Lieutenant Flemming did as they were told. They stayed out of the way but remained at the scene to offer their assistance. Special Agent Penny Adler had been told of the bombing at Detective Sullivan's home by the FBI's Bomb Technician. Penny stayed well out of the way, as told, as she approached the group that was remaining.

"You have any thoughts on this Sully?" She asked.

"Well, Reinstadt is at the top of my list of 'Who done-its.'" He replied confidently.

"I agree. I think you shook him up a little. You know the funny thing about your interview with him is that you were really coy. I think that frustrated him. After all, he was really pumping you for information." Penny surmised.

"I guess he felt I knew too much and was hiding it from him. At any rate, I'm sure he's our bomber." Sully added.

Samuel Jennings, the Detective III from CCS had approached the gathering of the lookey-loo investigators. He asked Sully if he had any thoughts as to why he had been targeted. Sully explained to Jennings the ongoing investigation that he had regarding the murder of Detective Ralph Doyle. Sully explained that the murder of Doyle was connected to a White Supremacist Group. A group that was also responsible for a series of homosexual murders in Griffith Park. Sully added that he had interviewed a member of the

Extremist Movement that may very well be behind all the murders. Sully explained that he believed that this is the person responsible for the bombing.

Jennings asked. "Can you tell me who it is?"

Sully answered, "Richard Reinstadt," Sully spelled out the last name for Jennings. "R-e-i-n-s-t-a-d-t."

Sully then offered a quick briefing for Jennings. "He is a long-time player in the Right Wing Extremist Movement. He's been a member of the Ku Klux Klan and the Aryan Nations. He's run with the Militia oddball and now we believe he is leading a group of the Neo-Nazi Skinheads."

"My guess is that you would like us to sit on this and let you guys run with things. Am I correct?" Asked Jennings.

"If you don't mind Sam," as Sully called him, "We are looking at several suspects. All at the same time, and all are involved in six homicides, now seven, if you count the stiff on my front lawn. I'll promise you this. I will not keep you out of the loop. You will be kept up to date on the overall investigation. Fair enough?" Sully asked.

Samuel Jennings agreed with Sully and truth be known, he was glad not to be saddled with the responsibility of another bombing investigation, especially one attached to a dead body.

It was now getting into the early evening hours. It was clear that the Sullivans would not be sleeping at home this night. Meg called her sister, Clara, and told her what had happened at their home. She told her sister that they might need to spend the next couple of nights with her and Robert. Clara told Meg that she would start preparing dinner. Before they hung up Meg asked.

"How's my little guy doing?"

"Shawn is fine. He and Robert are in the backyard playing." Clara told Meg.

"Robert is in the yard playing with a one-year-old? I'd love to see that." Meg interjected.

"Robert may be a Grandfather but when it comes to the little ones like Shawn, well, there just isn't really much difference in their ages. The little boy in Robert just comes out." Clara laughed.

CHAPTER XIV

THE SURVEILLANCE

A S IT WOULD TURN OUT, ALL THE RESEARCH AND preparation done Wednesday morning at Major Crimes Division would pay off. In reading Doyle's files, the team of investigators was able to at least find addresses for Franklyn Andrews and Keith Thomas. Unfortunately, no address was found for Justin Davis. Lieutenant Flemming was able to put together surveillance teams for both Andrews and Thomas. However, with the interruption the previous day and with the bombing at Sullivan's home, Flemming returned to work and worked into the late evening. The Lieutenant completed putting the surveillance packages together for the two skinheads. The surveillance of the two skinheads would commence Friday morning.

The teams were in position at the homes of Keith Thomas and Frankly Andrews at 6:00 a.m. It was 7:00 a.m. when Keith Thomas left his parent's home. Thomas was driving an older Ford pickup truck. Thomas drove directly to the home of Franklyn Andrews, arriving at 7:15 a.m. Andrews joined Thomas in the pickup and the pair drove to a small machine shop in the City of San Fernando. Both surveillance teams went with the two subjects. When they arrived at Wilson's machine shop, they couldn't help but notice the black, 1988 Chevy 4 door, parked there in the parking lot.

It was 7:30 a.m. when Thomas and Andrews entered the shop. It appeared that all three skinheads worked at the machine shop. Both surveillance teams took up appropriate positions. The first team would continue to surveil Keith and Franklyn, while the second team would standby to surveil Justin Davis as he departed work. They would stay on Davis until they were able to place him at a residence.

Sergeant Tim Campbell called Lieutenant Flemming on his cell phone to report what the teams had learned very early in the surveillance. The Sergeant reported that all three skinheads were together at what was most likely a work location. The Lieutenant was provided with the name of the business: "Wilson's Machine Shop" at 2460 San Fernando Road in the City of San Fernando.

Anthony Flemming went to work to learn what he could about the machine shop. With the help of Meg, they began making calls to the City of San Fernando, the San Fernando Chamber of Commerce and so on. Through the normal checks they found that Moses Wilson was the owner/operator of the machine shop. They were also able to learn that the work done in the machine shop was for the most part automotive: milling heads, boring engines... mostly high-performance engines.

They then began to focus on the owner operator Moses Wilson. As it turned out Moses was a black man in his mid-sixties. Moses was born in Shreveport, Louisiana. He never finished high school. Instead, he enlisted in the United States Navy at the age of 17. Moses Wilson was very handy with his hands and a miracle worker with engines. He served twenty years in the Navy, retiring at the rank of Chief Petty Officer. CPO, as they were called, is the most highly respected non-commissioned rank in the Navy.

Although serving his country, both on land and sea, Moses found time to March with Dr. Martin Luther King Jr., doing his part to bring civil rights to the forefront. Both Attorney Flemming and Meg thought it odd that these three White Supremacists would be earning a living by working for, not just a black man, but a black man that dedicated his life to the civil rights of all Black Americans.

Lieutenant Flemming contacted Sergeant Campbell and informed him of what they had learned about the machine shop and its owner. Flemming requested that Campbell have a member of his team make an entry into the business under the pretense of having work done to his engine to obtain an estimate for boring and stroking of a Chevy 350. Special instructions were to look around and make a mental picture of the location: Type of machinery, what type of work the skinheads were doing, etc. Flemming wanted every detail, right down to pictures and calendars hanging on the walls.

Sergeant Campbell briefed Detective Erik Santos and then sent him in. Santos was part of the second surveillance team standing by to surveil Justin Davis. Detective Santos entered the shop and was met at the front counter by Moses Wilson. After the usual "Hello" and "How can I help you" was out of the way, Santos explained.

"Yes Sir. I have a Chevy 350 that I am thinking about beefing up. I was wondering what it would cost me to bore and stoke it?"

Moses began to explain the services they offered as well as the costs involved. All the while Santos was surveying the room. On the walls were the normal shop calendars provided by Snap-on tools, NAPA and other suppliers of automotive parts. Santos could see what must have been the office used by Moses Wilson. On the wall were three photos of notables. First there was Dr. Martin Luther King, Jr. The second photo was of President John Fitzgerald Kenney and the third photo was of Desmond TuTu.

Detective Santos continued to nod as if acknowledging all that Moses was explaining to him. Santos then asked if it wouldn't be too much trouble if he could have a tour of the shop. Moses took Santos back into the work area. There he saw six employees: the three skinheads, two Hispanics and one Korean. Santos saw nothing on the walls other than tools and auto parts.

On the way back to the lobby area Santos commented to Moses.

"You sure are an equal employment opportunity employer. That's got to be one of the most diverse groups I've ever seen in one place."

Moses laughed, "Believe me. It's accidental. I didn't plan it. These boys just answered the ads as I put them in the paper is all."

Santos thought he could stretch his luck just a little more.

"Those white guys you got sure look a little eerie."

Moses laughed, "Yeah, well truth of the matter is, I think that they are Nazi's. Don't really know for sure. Don't give me any trouble and don't fight with the other boys working with me. And, to tell you the truth, those boys can handle the work I give them, and they do a good job of it. So, I let them be and that's that."

Santos told Moses that he would be in touch and left the shop.

Down in Fallbrook the FBI surveillance team had been set up on the residence of Richard Reinstadt. The agents were in position at 6:00 a.m. The team had sat on Reinstadt's home on Wednesday, but Reinstadt had not moved. They were hoping for more action today. They had no activity to report until 12:30 p.m., when Reinstadt departed his residence. He drove first to a Denny's Coffee Shop where he would have lunch. Reinstadt took a booth next to the window. Special Agent Victor Gwinn entered the Coffee Shop about two minutes later and took a seat at the lunch counter. Gwinn ordered a lunch salad and coffee. Reinstadt was enjoying a cheeseburger and onion rings when the hostess escorted a black family in to be seated in the booth next to Reinstadt.

Reinstadt jumped up from his seat and began yelling at the hostess in a heavy German accent. Gwinn had a hard time deciphering what Reinstadt was ranting and raving about. Gwinn could clearly make out the parts, "You don't think you're going to put these Niggers next to me!" Gwinn heard a few more things he could not understand and then heard, "If you want to ruin my lunch why stop at Niggers? Why not surround me with Jews as well?" Reinstadt then stormed out of the diner. Gwinn thought to himself, Reinstadt had just yelled his way out of paying for his lunch.

If nothing else, the event at Denny's proved two things: Reinstadt was in fact a White Supremacist filled with hate, and more importantly, he was extremely volatile. His confrontation with the hostess was a point in fact. Reinstadt was in her face. All the while staring down the black man who was there merely to dine with his family. It was as though Reinstadt was daring the man to do something. Gwinn thought Reinstadt was overcompensating for his shortness.

Reinstadt drove directly from Denny's to a Home Depot. Reinstadt went into the Home Depot taking a shopping basket with him. Special Agent Sandra Hernandez also entered the Home Depot. She also took a basket in with her. Sandra grabbed some light bulbs and threw them into her basket as she attempted to keep tables on Reinstadt. Reinstadt had just placed a small spool of electrical wire in his basket. Agent Hernandez did not see where Reinstadt had gotten the wire so she could not see what gauge wire that he had taken. She could only see that it was thinner than most of the other wire in the electronics area. Reinstadt next took three thermostats from the shelf and placed them in his basket before moving on to another area of the store. After Reinstadt was out of sight, Hernandez also grabbed one of the thermostats.

Reinstadt next went to the Plumbing Section. There he grabbed three twelve-inch by two-inch pipe nipples, six end caps, and a can of pipe dope. Hernandez entered the aisle from the opposite end of where Reinstadt was selecting his items. Hernandez selected some items for the purpose of repairing a sprinkler system. She then continued past Reinstadt noting the pipes and end caps in his basket.

Reinstadt's next stop in the store was the Hardware Section. Reinstadt stopped in front of the nails. He was holding a large box of carpet tacks as Hernandez passed him by. Hernandez stopped in front of the cabinet doorknobs and was looking at the selection when she caught Reinstadt out of the corner of her eye. He was placing the carpet tacks in his basket. As Reinstadt went to the check out clerk, Hernandez went down the aisle to the carpet tacks and read the label on the box. The box noted a 1000 tack quantity. Hernandez called out on her cell phone to the team leader to let him know that Reinstadt was done shopping and would be exiting Home Depot shortly.

Reinstadt left Home Dept and returned to his resident. Reinstadt took his goodies from the hardware store and entered the apartment. The surveillance team was set up on the residence until 6:00 p.m. There was no noted activity from 3:00 p.m., when Reinstadt returned home and 6:00 p.m. when the team went end of watch.

Special Agent Hernandez telephoned Agent Adler and briefed her on the day's events. Adler thought it would be best if the team went back up on Reinstadt Saturday morning at 6:00 a.m. Hernandez agreed and told Penny Adler that the team leader was already on the phone with agents from San Diego and had requested their services for Saturday. Hernandez related that they were being told that the team was on to something too hot to be abandoned.

Adler immediately called Sully, who himself was being briefed by Lieutenant Flemming and Meg. Sully had taken the day off to be at home when the contractor came to replace his front door and windows. Sully hated to put Penny off, but he was still on the house phone with Flemming and, of course, Meg. Sully explained this to Penny and promised to call her right back.

Flemming told Sully that all three subjects were still at the workplace. The two surveillance teams had been relieved by one fresh team. This new team would let Keith Thomas and Franklyn Andrews run free. They would stay with Justin Davis until he was bedded down, a term used for in for the night.

Sully called Agent Adler. He felt he had worthy news from the LAPD surveillance of Thomas and Andrews. Little did he know that what Penny had to report would blow his socks off. Penny answered excitedly with what she had to lay on Sully.

"Sully, that you? You are not going to believe what my guys came up with today."

Sully interrupted, "Yeah? Well I have some good stuff for you too. But what's the old saying? Ladies first."

Penny went right into it beginning with Reinstadts violent behavior at Denny's, including his racist remarks. She then told him that Reinstadt had driven from Denny's to a Home Depot. There she said they hit the jackpot. Penny told Sully that Reinstadt was observed by Agent Hernandez purchasing the following items: a spool of electrical wire, unknown small gauge, three thermostat control switches, (mercury type), three twelve inch nipples, (two inches in diameter), along with six end caps. And, the last item was a box of carpet tacks.

Sully was amazed at what the FBI surveillance team had learned in just one day. Sully thought that with what Reinstadt had done today that maybe they should stay with him tomorrow as well. Before Sully could suggest this to Agent Adler she added.

"Oh, and by the way Sully, my guys are going back up on Reinstadt tomorrow; maybe even Sunday."

"You're one step ahead of me," answered Sully. "Our day was very productive as well. Nothing as intriguing as yours, however, our teams had Keith Thomas and Franklyn Andrews hook up and go to work together. They work in a machine shop in San Fernando. And, guess what? Justin Davis works there as well. As of six o'clock they were all still at work. We have a fresh team on the work location now. They'll go with Justin when he leaves work. Maybe we'll get a residence address for the little dick head."

Penny told Sully that things were really moving fast with these guys. She told Sully that she was going to begin working on a search warrant for Reinstadt's apartment. She told Sully that the only thing that Reinstadt lacked to complete his explosive device was gun powder. She acknowledged that they had not yet seen him obtain flash bulbs or 9-volt batteries. However, if they see him take gun powder into his residence where the pipes and end caps are, then the courts would agree that he is in possession of the components to construct an explosive device. This would be enough for a search warrant and she wanted to be ready.

"Well you never know what tomorrow will bring," Sully said in agreement.

All and all it turned out to be a very good day all around. Flemming's surveillance teams gained a great deal of intelligence on their surveillance and the FBI team on Reinstadt hit one out of the park. And, as for Sully? Well he got his house back in order. Although this night too would be spent with Meg's sister and brother-in-law, he knew that he, Meg and Young Shawn would hopefully be back home Saturday night in time to enjoy the rest of the weekend.

It was 7:30 p.m. when Moses locked up his machine shop. Just as his employees pulled out of the parking lot Justin Davis was the last to leave after waiting for his boss, Moses Wilson, to get into his car. After saying good night to Moses, Justin drove directly to the Golden State Freeway or Interstate 5, as it is officially called. Justin went south to the 170 toward Hollywood. The 170 merges with US 101. Justin took the 101 to the Western off ramp. He parked in front of Danny's Peep Show at Western Avenue and Santa Monica Blvd. Justin entered the sex shop and walked directly over to the rack of dildos. Officer Cynthia Gomez entered a short time later and began to browse. Justin was not in the sex shop for more than five minutes when he took his purchase to the register. Officer Gomez approached the counter and eyeing both the fifteen-inch dildo and Justin remarked,

"That's pretty big stud. How about you? You hung big boy?"

"Get the fuck away from me you Mexican whore!" Justin lashed out. "This is pure white!" He yelled as he gestured to himself with both hands. "This only comes in pure white!"

While Justin went into his fit, Officer Gomez had an opportunity to look at the dildo atop the counter. She made note of the swastika located on the head of the rubber penis. Justin finished with his purchase and began to storm out of the shop. Cynthia could not resist one last quip.

"Did you want some KY to go with that? It may make entry easier when you sit on it!"

Justin flipped her the finger as he exited. Justin got into his car and drove back to the San Fernando Valley. Justin parked in front of a duplex at 1821 Pinewood in Sunland. He entered the front unit and the interior lights were turned on. The team set up on Justin's residence and notified Sully of Justin's trip to Danny Peep Show Sex Shop and his return to the residence, which they now knew. Sully was also told about the purchase of the fifteen-inch dildo with the swastika.

Sully was concerned by the purchase of the dildo. He felt that the skinheads must be preparing for their next victim. Sully instructed the team to stay on Justin until 2:00 a.m. before going end of watch, and only if they believed Justin had gone to bed, lights out.

CHAPTER XV

FAIRY LANE DRIVE

T HE LAPD SURVEILLANCE TEAM WAS IN POSITION AT the home of Justin Davis. A duplex at 1821 Pinewood, located in the northeast corner of the San Fernando Valley. The decision had been made by Sully and Lieutenant Flemming to stay with the dildo twenty-four hours a day now. Until the skinheads put it into play, so to speak, they would put two teams on this. The first team would begin at 6:00 a.m. and be relieved by the second team at 6:00 p.m. The night team would be assisted by an air unit. Sully and Special Agent Adler would make similar plans for the surveillance of Richard Reinstadt.

Saturday morning would begin for Justin Davis with a two-mile jog. At an easy pace Justin jogged to Vic's Gym. The gym itself was small and situated in a strip mall. The gym contained a ring for sparring, as well as a small area for weightlifting. Davis spent almost a full hour lifting weights. He followed that up with twenty minutes of jumping rope. Members of the surveillance team watching Davis through the large front window described Justin's jump roping as Rocky Balboa like. Justin then went to work on a punching bag. He would jab at the bag all the while bobbing and weaving. Justin danced around the bag in this fashion for just more than a half hour.

After spending the next twenty minutes on a speed bag, Justin climbed into the ring. He put on boxing gloves which were laced for him by the gym's operator, Vic Monroe. Vic put a boxing head protector on Justin, and he was ready to spar with his opponent. While Vic, acting as referee and trainer for both corners, the two boys sparred three-minute rounds, with a one-minute rest period between rounds. The surveillance officers were amazed at just how well Justin handled himself in the ring.

After the go-around in the ring, Justin headed home. This time he would walk, sort of a cool down if you will. The surveillance team learned a lot about Justin on this morning. It was now obvious as to just how fit Justin was. Not only was this skinhead strong, but he had lasting endurance. It was also quite clear that if Justin was to resist arrest, he was going to be a handful to handle.

It was 11:15 a.m. when Justin returned to his residence. Justin would enjoy a long hot shower to ease the tightness in his muscles after a long hard workout. After freshening up Justin would again leave his home. This time he would take his car. It was a short drive, just eight blocks to Matt's Burgers and Malts. Justin sat alone in the outside patio area and ate lunch. He was an extraordinary slow eater. Perhaps a disciplined eating regiment acquired through his physical fitness training. Although Justin was eating slowly and chewing his food thoroughly, he was still wolfing down a triple cheeseburger, French fries, and a thick chocolate malt. Best guess, slightly more than a thousand calories in one sitting.

The surveillance team itself was now hungry. But there was no time for them to grab a bite. Not yet anyway. Justin finally completed savoring his fast food cuisine and departed Matt's. Justin then drove to the Los Angeles City Library, the Sunland-Tujunga Branch. It was 2:00 p.m. when Justin entered the Library. Janet Brown, one of the surveillance officers entered the Library at 2:15 p.m. She found Justin seated at a table and apparently reading. Janet selected a magazine, one of those chick-type magazines with the surveys on sex. You know, the ones women are always trying to answer. The ones that want to know if you know what your man needs to get him off and fall deeply in love with you.

Janet sat down at the adjoining table and directly across from Justin. This afforded her a clear view at the book Justin was reading. The book was entitled: <u>U.S. History and the American Revolution.</u> Justin was doing more than just looking at the pictures and illustrations. He was reading and taking notes. Janet thought to herself that this confused Neo-Nazi was really into American History. Well, maybe at least the Revolution. She was curious to know what it was that Justin was writing on the notepad.

Janet left her magazine at her place at the table. She went into the Ladies Room and when she was sure there was no one else there she called her team leader and provided an update. She related that Justin was brushing up on the American Revolution. But that she couldn't tell what he was making notes on. It was now 5:00 p.m. and the team would soon be relieved by the night watch crew. Janet suggested that she approach Justin and engage him in conversation. Maybe learn what it is that has his full attention.

When Janet returned to her magazine, she removed it from the tabletop and relocated herself to Justin's table. Janet sat down and began to speak in a whisper. After all, this was the Public Library and talking was frowned upon.

"Hi. I don't mean to disturb you, but I am impressed."

Justin whispered in an inquisitive reply, "Impressed? About what?"

Janet explained, "Well here I am reading a meaningless magazine, taking a quiz that proves I don't know how to fulfill a man's dreams or much less please him, while you study history."

Justin now a little embarrassed responded, "Listen, I'm not some bookworm Geeky kinda guy. I just really have an interest in my country's history. Especially how our forefathers founded and shaped our country's beginning."

Janet played interested, "I couldn't help noticing you taking notes. I though maybe you were in college or something. You know, doing homework."

Justin played into her hand. "No, I am writing down portions of the Bill of Rights. You know, things that our Founding Fathers wanted to guarantee each of us. Things that ZOG is now trying to deprive us of."

"ZOG?" Questioned Janet.

"Yeah, you've heard of ZOG haven't you?" Justin asserted.

"No. I am sorry. Should I have?" Janet countered.

"You poor naive girl. ZOG is the initials of the current government. It means Zionist Occupied Government. You see that Zions," Justin paused as he could tell that Janet didn't understand what a Zionist was. "Jews, the Jews have taken over the government." Justin was beginning to become a little animated and louder as well.

"Shush," Janet insisted. Keep it down a little or they'll make us leave. Now go ahead. Tell me what the Jews are doing to take the rights away from you that are guaranteed in the Bill of Rights.

Justin began to explain, "Well, it's a collection of a lot of things actually. One of the biggest intrusions to our rights is gun control. The Constitution guarantees our rights to bear arms. This was a right given to us to protect ourselves from a tyrannical government. ZOG is making us register our guns. So that they know who has them. So, when the time comes, they can go around and collect them."

"Why would they want to do that?" Janet asked dumbfounded.

"You don't see the big picture," Justin said sounding a little frustrated. "Look, I don't have time to explain it all to you here in the Library in just a few minutes. Here," Justin handed Janet a slip of paper with his name and phone number, "Call me and I'll invite you to an educational meeting of the Guardians of Israel."

"The Guardians of Israel?" Janet questioned. "I thought you said that the Jews were at the heart of, ah what did you call it? ZOG? Yes, ZOG."

Justin answered, "Okay, this one last point and then I need to go. It's already six o'clock. Jews are evil. They are the Children of Satan. That state in the Middle East that the Jews call Israel is Palestine. The United States is the true Israel and white Christians are the true Israelites, the chosen people. I know it's hard to follow if you haven't had the proper teaching. Call me. I'll see to it that you get the straight story. Listen, I have got to go now."

Justin returned his book and grabbed his notes. The Relief Team was already in place and ready to take Justin away from the Library. Janet walked out and handed the note that Justin had given her to Officer Frank Hauss, who was keeping the surveillance activity log.

"He actually gave you his name and phone number?" Frank questioned.

"Yeah. I'm a pretty smooth talker you know." Janet replied in that snobby Valley Girl tone.

"Well, do you have a date with the Nazi?" Frank questioned.

"Frank. You're not jealous?" Janet jabbed back.

"You two aren't planning to spar all night, are you? Because the rest of us would like to go home. Janet just tell Frank what he needs for the log and let's call it a day shall we?" Commanded Sergeant Vernon, the Team Leader.

Janet briefed the team on what had taken place in the Library with Justin. She almost recited the conversation between herself and Justin Davis word for word. Frank wrote it down the best he could so that it could be included in the activity log for the day's surveillance. Frank thought to himself that it seemed to him that on the days he kept the log, the surveillance was overly active and on the days another team member was responsible for the log, they did nothing. Why was it he couldn't do the log on a zero-event day?

The Day Watch Team went end of watch. Their plan was to be back at 0:600 hours in the morning at Justin's home. Little did they know that the Night Watch Team was going to be knee-deep in shit tonight and that Sunday would bring them a day of rest.

The Night Watch Team was supervised by Sergeant Timothy O'Hara, a red-headed Irishman. Sergeant Tim, as the troops called him, stood about six feet, two inches. He was thin in stature and resembled Conan O'Brien of the late-night show on NBC. Sergeant Tim's team took Justin Davis back to his residence on Pinewood. The Team would sit idle until 10:00 p.m. when Keith Thomas and Franklyn Andrews would arrive together in the pickup truck driven by Keith Thomas.

The two Skinheads were seen entering Justin's residence as Justin himself opened the door. The three Skinheads would exit the duplex unit at 11:15 p.m. The surveillance team would have no way of knowing that the three had been throwing back several long necks. Apparently, in an effort to build up enough courage to kill another homosexual in the hills of Griffith Park.

The three Neo-Nazi's loaded into Justin's 1988 Chevy Impala and headed to Hollywood. The surveillance team would tail them through the San Fernando Valley, mostly on major boulevards and of course freeways. Justin would eventually take US 101 to Highland. Highland passes through the heart of Hollywood. The trio of harmdoers would eventually arrive at La Brea and Santa Monica. To the Skinheads, Santa Monica Avenue between La Brea in the City of Los Angeles and west, through the City of West Hollywood was known as: "Fairy Lane Drive."

This is where you went to find a young male prostitute. The young boys, ages sixteen to twenty-three or maybe a young looking twenty-six year old, peddled their ass to older males looking for "Brokeback Mountain" type one night stands. The Vice Cops in Hollywood referred to these young men as "Bun Boys". A lot of these young men came to Hollywood seeking fame and fortune in the movies. Unfortunately, they found out that fame and fortune are out of their reach. There are no overnight movie idols in the reality of Hollywood.

Several young men, like their female counterparts, end up doing pornography. In the world of heterosexual porn there is a big demand for young, sweet, teenage looking girls. This, on the other hand does not hold true for young boyish looking men. There is however a big demand for the boyish hard body types in guy-on-guy film in the porn industry. Many of these Bun Boys on Santa Monica Boulevard never had homosexual urges before arriving in Hollywood. They were sucked into gay porn for survival and false promises by porn producers; promises to put them into legitimate features. The Bun Boys would appear in two or three guy-on-guy productions. The producer would then tire of them and cast them aside, replacing them with a younger and fresher face. All that was left for them to survive was as a street prostitute.

The life of a Bun Boy was dangerous. It was a life on the street, hooking up with strange men. A good-looking Bun Boy, who did not bulk at a requested sexual act, could make a great deal of money in one night. Most of the John's looking for a young man for boy-toy sex were well off. Some were married men with children at home. They loved their wives and enjoyed sex with them, yet still had uncontrollable urges to get it on with a young man.

The sex varied from John to John. Some men wanted an exchange of just oral sex. Some wanted to fuck the Bun Boy, while others wanted to be fucked by the Bun Boy. Then there was the John that wanted to do it all, all night long.

Elliot James Burton was twenty-six and considered old for a Bun Boy. Elliot, however, could easily pass for a naïve sixteen-year-old boy. He did not look a day over his sixteenth birthday. Elliot was born and raised in Littlerock, Arkansas. His southern accent soft and refined, it had an almost elegant tone to it.

Elliot came to Hollywood, like so many others, to make it into the movies. Elliot, though, was an out of the closet homosexual. In high school, Elliot was out in the open with his preference for men over women. Elliot's dream for life in Hollywood was not for a leading character role. Elliot merely wanted to be a dancer in a hit musical.

To date, the only movies Elliot had been in were gay porn. He was in fact homosexual, so he did not have that appearance or reluctance that most other Bun Boys displayed. For this reason, Elliot had more longevity in the porn industry than the other newcomers to Hollywood.

The three Skinheads cruised Fairy Lane Drive until 1:00 a.m. when they spotted Elliot James Burton on the north sidewalk of Santa Monica, a block and a half west of La Brea. Justin pulled his car to the curb and parked next to where Elliot was standing. Justin thought that having the three of them in the car just might scare Elliot off. So Justin suggested that all three of them get out and engage the unsuspecting queer in conversation.

"Hi there," Justin remarked as the three Skinheads approached.

"My name is Justin, and these are my buddies, Franklyn and Keith."

"Hi there. I'm Elliot," he returned their greeting.

"Look. I know this is weird for you, there being the three of us and all. The fact is, we were looking to party if you know what I mean?" Justin said trying to break the ice and set Elliot at ease.

"How much partying you talking about?" Asked Elliot.

Keith jumped in, "How much party can we get?"

Elliot didn't feel comfortable with the trio of partygoers. But it had been a dud of a night and he thought a party with three horny, well-hung studs could net him at least a thousand dollars.

"Look, there are three of you. That's a big task to take on. But I'll tell you what I'll do. I'll see to it that you each have the time of your life for a grand. How does that sound? A grand time for a grand," Elliot proposed his deal.

Justin, Keith and Franklyn huddled together. Franklyn popped his head up, winked at Elliot and then returned to the conversation in the huddle. The huddle broke and Justin agreed.

"Okay, you have a deal. We'll load up and drive up to a lover's lane spot on the hill. We'll bring you back here afterwards. That work for you?"

Elliot agreed to go with them. The surveillance team would stay on Justin's car so long as they remained on the busier streets. However, when they drove into the residential area in the hills off of Los Feliz, it was time for the air unit to take over. The air unit kept watch on Justin's car right up to the point where the car drove up the service road at the end of Maple Street leading to the water tank.

What neither the air unit nor the ground units could detect was the horror being experienced by Elliot as their drive progressed from Fairy Lane Drive to the base of the Griffith Park hills. Elliot was in the back seat with Justin and Franklyn while Keith drove. Elliot sat between the two of them when suddenly Justin grabbed Elliot around the head and pulled him downward toward his lap. At the same time Franklyn hurriedly placed duct tape over his mouth. Both Justin and Franklyn wrestled Elliot's hands behind his back and Franklyn taped them together using the roll of duct tape.

Justin then began to slowly and methodically cut Elliot's clothing away from his body. Justin, all the while telling Elliot that he, Keith and Franklyn were God's Messengers. They were sent by God to ensure the survival of a heterosexual, white world. The fear was clearly easy to see in Elliot's eyes. As each item of clothing was cut away from Elliot, Justin would taunt him repeatedly. Justin ran his hunting knife over the skin of Elliot's unclothed body parts. Franklyn finished cutting away Elliot's designer jeans leaving him now, in only his underwear.

As Franklyn began playing with a pair of vise grips only eight inches away from Elliot's face, Justin slipped his knife under Elliot's underpants. Elliot could feel the cold steel of the blade scrape by his penis. Justin then jerked on the huge knife cutting away at the undergarment at the left leg. Justin slid the knife down Elliot's pants once again. The right side was then sliced open allowing the briefs to be pulled away, completely exposing Elliot.

Franklyn was first to gasp.

"Holy shit! That's one big cock." Franklyn looked at Justin and added. "I'll bet he's as big as our Swastika dildo!"

Justin gave an ugly sneer at Elliot and yelled, "Why is it you fags always have the biggest cocks?"

Justin, in an angry rage grabbed the vise grips from Franklyn and clamped them down on the head of Elliot's penis. Not too tight. Not yet anyway. It was just tight enough to cause a slight pain.

As Keith drove up the park service road to the water tank, the air unit had activated its infrared light. The air unit kept the ground units informed of just what they were observing.

"They are getting out of the vehicle which is parked well behind the water tank. Two subjects are pulling a nude body out from the rear seat of the vehicle. It appears that the nude male has his hands bound behind his back." Was the broadcast from the air unit observer?

It was at this point that Sergeant O'Hara gave the go. The team members were out of their vehicles now moving up the service road on foot. As they moved slowly around the water tank, they could hear the muffled screams of Elliot Burton. They could also hear the snickers and threats of the three Skinheads.

As the police officers rounded the water tank to the point where they observed the Skinheads with their helpless victim, the officers took action. Flashlights illuminated the suspects and orders to "freeze" were bellowed out by the officers. Franklyn Andrews and Keith Thomas froze in a puddle of their own urine.

Justin Davis, on the other hand, took off running. Sergeant O'Hara and Officer DeShawn Jackson gave chase. O'Hara was no match for Justin who was without a doubt in top physical condition. DeShawn, however, was a different story. A graduate of Locke High School in Los Angeles, DeShawn was a track star. In fact, he was such a standout, that it earned him a scholarship to the University of Southern California. DeShawn ran track at USC for four years. He joined the LAPD after graduation.

DeShawn caught up with Justin and gave him a shove knocking Justin to the ground. Justin, slightly scrapped up by his collision with the asphalt of Maple Street, stood and brushed himself off. He looked at his opponent and began to dance around as he did earlier in the ring when sparring.

"You're going down nigger." Justin proclaimed.

Not only was DeShawn a star athlete in track, he was also a Golden Gloves Champion. DeShawn continued his love for boxing by competing in the Police and Fire World Games annually. The round between Justin and DeShawn lasted less than three seconds before Justin had his bell rung.

Sergeant O'Hara, out of breath, caught up to Officer Jackson, and panting he uttered, "Good job." He then dropped to his knees and cuffed Justin.

CHAPTER XVI

I'M SORRY

THE ARREST OF THE THREE SKINHEADS WOULD PROVE to be the break they were looking for in the murders of Detective Ralph Doyle and his informant, Amanda Cavanaugh. Sergeant Timothy O'Hara would call in a couple of black and white units to transport the suspects to the Hollywood Station. Of course, with instructions to keep each of the suspects separated. An RA Unit from the Los Angeles Fire Department would be dispatched to care for the medical needs of Elliot Thurton. Elliot would be treated at the scene as his injuries did not require hospitalization. The emergency medical team assigned to the RA (Rescue Ambulance) was more than capable of tending to Elliot's needs. The Fire Paramedics were even able to provide Elliot with hospital type smokes to cover his nudity.

Elliot was held at the crime scene to assist the surveillance team in piecing together the evidence that they would eventually collect. The first thing that was recovered was of course the vise grips that had been securely fastened to the head of Elliot's penis. Sergeant O'Hara did the honors. As he began to remove the gripping tool, O'Hara questioned with a slight chuckle, "Tell me son, is this device giving you a slight woody? Or are you just hung like a stallion?"

Elliot appreciated O'Hara's humoristic tone and responded with a grin. "Sergeant, tools don't turn me on!"

If you were to count the duct tape used to cover Elliot's mouth and bound his hands together, the vice grips would be considered the third item of evidence recovered. The A team member found the hunting knife. It had been dropped at the rear corner panel on the driver's side of the car. This is the location where the officers had observed Justin Davis grasping a hard hold on Elliot. Elliot was shown the knife and asked if he knew who had it. Elliot was able to tell them that it was the property of the skinhead that had run down the hill. They naturally noted that the item of evidence had been abandoned at the scene by Suspect Justin Davis.

Inside the car and in plain view of the front passenger seat of Justin's Chevy were several leather straps and what appeared to be a branding iron with the Hermaphrodite Symbol at one end. There was also a portable blow torch on the seat - approximately a one-half gallon canister model, and of course the Swastika cock. Sergeant O'Hara felt confident that his team had collected enough evidence to book the suspects for the four unsolved homosexual murders in Griffith Park.

O'Hara called Lieutenant Anthony Flemming and briefed him as to the evening's events and arrests. Flemming called Sully at home. It was now 4:30 a.m. on Sunday morning. Sully would call Kathy Burgess and ask her to meet him at Hollywood Station. Sully would not have to awaken Meg. She woke up as he did with the call from Flemming.

The only ones left to call and wake up before dawn on Sunday morning were of course Clara and Robert. They would once again be called upon to look after Little Shawn.

It was just before 6:00 a.m. when the team of investigators met at Hollywood Station. The Day Watch surveillance team was instead sent back to the residence at 1821 Pinewood. They would need to secure the location until a search warrant could be served. The team met with Sergeant O'Hara and was briefed in full as to the events that unfolded during the surveillance. This included statements made by the victim, Elliot James Burton, and the evidence recovered by the surveillance team. Sully thought for a moment while he mentally processed what O'Hara had told him. After a brief pause of silence Sully began.

"Did your people complete the crime report for this victim... what was his name? Ah, oh yes, Elliot Burton?"

O'Hara responded, "They are with Elliot now and doing just that."

"Okay," continued Sully. "Let's make this a kidnapping and let's book all three suspects for the open charge of kidnap. Your team can complete the crime and arrest reports and book the suspects. We will begin putting together a search warrant for the Pinewood residence. The other dip-shits live with their parents, so I would not expect to find the evidence of the murders at their place."

Kathy Burgess hesitantly asked, "What about questioning the skinheads?"

Sully responded. "Okay, here is my thought on talking to these guys. So far, we have them for kidnapping. What we know is their fifth murder victim. True, we have leather straps, a branding iron and one huge pink rubber dildo with a Swastika on the head. What we don't have are the right ears of the four queers. I want the evidence that ensures an indictment for murder. Then we have the leverage to squeeze them about Doyle and Cavanaugh."

Fleming jumped in, "It's obvious that if you find the ears, you'll find Doyle's finger. Cavanaugh's too."

Sully wasn't so sure that Justin would have the fingers of his friend Ralph Doyle and the informant Amanda Cavanaugh. He corrected Lieutenant Fleming, "I don't think so Lieutenant. I don't believe the skinheads did the murders of Doyle and Cavanaugh alone. I am banking on Richard Reinstadt as the asshole that put those two homicides together. If I'm right, then it would be Reinstadt holding the trophy fingers as mementos and not Justin."

"I see your point Detective." Fleming conceded.

They then began to write their affidavit for a search warrant for 1821 Pinewood, Unit A, the residence of Justin Davis. Sully called the District Attorney's Office Command Post. Sully talked first to a D.A. Investigator and provided him with a very guarded outline of the investigation. Sully was proficient at spouting out sketchy details, while at the same time convincing the listener that his probable cause was concrete and unshakeable. It took Sully less than two minutes to talk the D.A. Investigator into calling Deputy District Attorney Jerry Levin at home.

Sully was patched through to Jerry, and for Jerry, Sully laid it all out. Jerry told Sully that he could meet him at the Criminal Courts Building downtown in forty-five minutes. Kathy Burgess was putting together the finishing touches on the affidavit and would transfer it to a disc. The entire team, Sully, Meg, Kathy and Fleming would load up into one vehicle. They would drive to the District Attorney's Office in the Criminal Courts Building. In hand they would have a compact disc with the Affidavit and five hard copies printed out for review and most likely a debate. Attorney's loved to tear things apart, especially documents prepared by cops. An Attorney was never more threatened than when a cop put together an Affidavit for a Search Warrant that was written with more insight and depth of eloquence than the attorney could himself accomplish.

Jerry Levin, on the other hand, was not as intimidated by proficiency. Jerry was a seasoned Prosecutor and was not so threatened by Detectives that were capable of enlightening him. Oh, Jerry would read over the Affidavit thoroughly and from time to time make minute suggestions for changes here and there, but as far as Jerry was concerned if a document was complete and well written he would not argue for these suggestions.

Jerry only noted a couple of minor flaws in the Affidavit. Nothing was critical to the credibility of the Affidavit. Just minor errors were noted. Once those were corrected, Jerry began putting the Search Warrant together. He also made a quick call to the D.A. Command Post and told the investigator on duty to find him a Judge. Preferably in the North San Fernando Valley area of Los Angeles.

Jerry added, "Tell him he will be signing a Search Warrant for a residence."

It was 10:00 a.m. when the team arrived at Judge Walter Barnes' home in Porter Ranch. Porter Ranch is an upscale area of Los Angeles located in the foothills bordering the north end of the San Fernando Valley. Judge Barnes read both the Affidavit and Search Warrant. He looked at Sully and remarked, "Everything here looks to be in order Detective. You figure you'll find these ears you're looking for?"

Sully admitted, "Don't know for sure your Honor. But if we do, you can bet we'll make our suspect choke on 'em."

"You know, you look very familiar. Have I had you in my court before?" Judge Barnes asked.

"Don't think so your Honor. I've spent my entire career in the south end of town." Sully answered.

The team was just exiting the Judge's home when Judge Barnes recalled. "I know, you're right. You haven't been in my court. I saw you on the news about a year ago. You had a major case involving the big shot attorney Edward Masey. The slime that set up all the murders of expectant mothers so that he could sell off their babies to his rich clients."

Sully smiled, "Yes sir. That was me." As he humbly admitted.

"Good job Detective. Hope to see you on the evening news with this one as well." The Judge remarked as he waved goodbye to the foursome.

It was 11:30 a.m. when Sully and his crew arrived at the 1821 Pinewood duplex. Sergeant Vernon's surveillance team had secured the residence awaiting the Search Warrant. Vernon informed the investigators. Actually, he was directing his comments to Lieutenant Fleming. Sergeant Vernon did work for the Lieutenant and although Sully was the lead Detective, he really didn't feel slighted. After all, Fleming was a Lieutenant and the fact is, his career with the Los Angeles Police Department dated back to the era of Chief William H. Parker.

Sergeant Vernon reported that his team arrived at the Justin Davis residence at 5:30 a.m. and no one had entered or left the residence during their watch.

Sully, along with Fleming and Vernon, approached the front door. Vernon used his night stick to rap on the front door causing a loud and pronounced racket. Sully yelled out. "Police Officers. We have a Search Warrant for the premises!"

There was no answer from within and there was no ruckus about indicating anyone was scurrying within. Sully looked at Vernon and questioned, "Sergeant. Who in your unit has the strongest foot?"

"That would be Michaels." Vernon responded.

"Is it his turn to kick a door?" Sully followed.

"On this team it's always his turn," insured Vernon.

"Michael, bring your boot up here." Yelled Sergeant Vernon.

Michaels trotted up the driveway to the front porch. The Officer was a Behemoth six foot-six inches in height. Sully guessed he tipped the scales at a good two hundred and ninety pounds or so. His fourteen EEE boot was nature's battering ram. Vernon stood in front of Officer Michaels. Looking up, of course as he instructed, "You are going to have to kick open the door. Try not to put your foot through this one Okay?"

"Yes Sergeant." Michaels responded in a deep voice that penetrated the human body with each syllable, causing a vibrating effect.

Lieutenant Fleming held the screen door open and to the side as he cautioned Michaels.

"Now son, concentrate on what you're doing. You don't want to put your big ass clod stomper through the door and get it stuck there. And, you surely don't want to lose your balance and fall flat on your ass in front of your partners and embarrass yourself. Or worse, embarrass the Department in front of all the onlookers that have now gathered to watch you on this momentous occasion. Okay, you ready? Any time now son. We are waiting."

Michaels knew the Lieutenant was fucking with his mind. But the fact was, there were a lot of people now watching him. And, the truth of the matter is that Michaels had gotten stuck when his foot went through a door on one other occasion. Now it's true that he had not ever lost his balance kicking a door or ended up on his ass. He had known of times when this had happened to other police officers. Sully could see the fear of embarrassment now on Michaels' face. Sully pointed to a spot on the door just below the doorknob.

"Kick it here. It will open to your command and you'll be the kick ass cop of the hour."

Michaels kicked the door at the point Sully instructed and the door flew open splintering the door jam. Michaels actually drew a cheer from the crowd that had gathered. One person had actually yelled out, "Okay big foot. Way to go man!"

Meg and Kathy Burgess joined Sully and Lieutenant Fleming as they entered the duplex apartment. Inside they found the apartment to be quite small. The living room was a cramped eleven foot by ten-foot room. There was a tiny kitchen and one small bedroom. The bathroom had a tub shower combination.

The living room had a sofa, coffee table and one floor lamp. The room was virtually clean. No papers, magazines or trash lying about. The kitchen, on the other hand, was a mess. There were dirty dishes both in the sink and on the counter. The cabinets were mostly boxes of cereal and cans of soup. The refrigerator was a seventeen cubic foot Hotpoint. Small, but almost too big for this kitchen. It contained a quart of milk, butter, a loaf of bread, a pack of individual cheese slices and, of course, several bottles of beer. Meg opened the freezer section above the refrigerator. In it she found three ice trays and four small sandwich bags. In the bags were items wrapped in aluminum foil. Meg brought the items to the attention of the others.

The four sandwich bags were removed from the freezer and placed on the coffee table in the living room: the only uncluttered surface nearby. Sully opened the first bag and removed the foil wrapped item. They were not shocked by their discovery. The human ear was a piece of evidence they had hoped to find. The other three packages also proved to be human ears. All four were right ears. All four had puncture marks for pierced earrings. They were a little disappointed that they did not find the right index fingers belonging to Detective Ralph Doyle or his informant, Amanda Cavanaugh.

Sully never really believed that the finger of his friend, nor the finger of the informant, would be found at the duplex apartment of Justin Davis. Sully was none the less disappointed. After all, if they had found the fingers, they would be that much closer to truly solving Doyle's murder. Sully was now more than ever convinced that Richard Reinstadt held the missing fingers as his own personal trophies.

Before continuing the search, Sully informed Sergeant Vernon that they had recovered four human ears. Sully asked Vernon to request the Los Angeles County Coroner's Office to respond and take possession of the human body parts.

The search of the residence of Justin Davis continued with the bedroom. It would be in the bedroom of Davis that the team of investigators would learn the darkest secret of Justin Davis. Dozens of pornographic magazines were located in the bedroom. But these were male on male homosexual publications. The television and DVD player sat atop of a cabinet. Inside the cabinet they found no less than sixty DVD's. Each one of them were clearly male homosexual pornography. Next to the bed was a nightstand. In the drawer of that nightstand were two tubes of KY jelly along with several butt plugs and dildos.

"He's queer. Justin Davis is queer!" This is our in. This is how we get Mr. Davis to open up and tell us in detail about each of the murders."

Lieutenant Fleming questioned with some doubt, "How do you think you're going to get to him? Just by telling him you know he's gay?"

"No. He's going to talk to ensure that we keep his secret from his skinhead buddies. He knows what they'll do to him if they find out he's as queer as the poor sons of bitches they tortured and murdered in Griffith Park. Trust me. He'll talk." Sully said with confidence.

They finished their search of Justin's residence. The Coroner collected the ears the team had discovered. Gathering Justin's collection of gay porn, they began their drive back to the Hollywood Police Station to begin interviewing the three skinheads.

Kathy Burgess was reviewing the photos that she had taken with a digital camera. The photos depicted their search of Justin's residence from start to finish. Kathy, after viewing the digital images of the ears remarked, "Sully, the shots I took of the four ears are really impressive."

Sully responded, "When we get to Hollywood you can download the photos and make 8 x 10 copies of each ear for me."

Meg now curious asked, "What do you need with 8 x 10 photos of each ear?"

Sully explained, "I intend to leave those photos on top of the table in the interview room. Then I am going to have Justin brought into the room, alone, with nobody to interrupt his concentration. I want him to sit there and stare at those photos for a good ten minutes. For him it will seem like an hour our so. When I finally enter the room, I'll throw his gay porn on the table."

Lieutenant Fleming could see where Sully was headed. "You know Sully I knew you were a good detective. But, just how good you were was still up in the air. Now I think, that is if I'm reading you correctly, you are a brilliant Detective! If this goes your way, you'll have this Justin kid in tears in less than ten minutes time."

Sully laughed, "That's the plan. I just hope I can get him to stop bawling long enough to spill his guts. I need him to tell all he knows about what happened to the four victims in the park. But more importantly, I need him to implicate Reinstadt in the murders of Doyle and Cavanaugh.

The team arrived at the Hollywood Station. Kathy Burgess and Meg went to the computer room to print out the 8 x 10 photos of the four ears. Anthony Fleming went to arrange the interview room. Sully was sifting through the box of magazines and DVD's. Sully was selecting those publications and items that most depicted the epitome of gay sex.

Sully was just about done with the task at hand when his cell phone rang. It was Special Agent Adler. Sully had tried to reach her earlier to let her know of the arrest of the three skinheads. When he was unable to each her, he contacted the Duty Agent at the FBI and left word for her to contact him.

"Penny. Wow I've been trying to reach you. We hit it big here. Our three skinheads were out late last night capering. They grabbed their fifth victim last night and drove him to the Griffith Park location." Sully was explaining.

"What happened? Did they kill another one?" Penny questioned. She was so excited she was pressing Sully to get to the end of his briefing.

"No. They didn't get the chance to kill this one. Our surveillance team took them down at just the right time." Sully satisfied her curiosity.

"That's good Sully. Have you talked to them yet?" Agent Adler asked. Sully then told Agent Adler of the initial arrest and all the evidentiary details that went with it. Sully followed this up with the search of Justin Davis' residence, the four ears found in the freezer and, of course, the discovery that Davis himself was homosexual. Penny was surprised to learn that Justin was gay.

"Do you think he was striking out at his own homosexuality by killing other gays?"

Sully paused for a moment and answered, "Quite frankly, I don't give a shit what psychosomatic excuse his defense team wants to offer up. At this point I play to use his queerness to get him talking!"

Agent Adler told Sully that she was in Fallbrook with the surveillance team. She added that Reinstadt had not been out of his apartment all day. Before concluding the phone call she told Sully that the cell phone service in the area was poor and that was the reason she did not get his message earlier. Sully had figured as much and before hanging up told Penny that he was sure that the fingers belonging to Ralph Doyle and Amanda Cavanaugh would be found in the freezer at Reinstadt's apartment. Sully told Agent Adler that he would know more after his talk with Justin.

The interview room had been prepared. There were four 8 x 10 photographs atop the table, each one depicting the ear of its previous owner's Gerald Clark, Richard Black, Peter Washington, and Gregory James Jefferson. Justin Davis was led into the interrogation room by the jailer. Actually, the interrogation room is old school. The terminology has been softened, made more politically correct. It is now called the interview room. This has a more touchy-feely flow to it. Interrogation room is harsh and makes one think of the old rubber hose used to beat a confession out of a suspect.

Justin sat down at the table. Sully, Meg, Kathy Burgess and the Lieutenant watched through a two-way mirror. Justin began looking at the photographs as he shuffled them back and forth looking at one and then the other over and over again with no certain pattern. As they watched through the mirror, they could see the tears well up in Justin's eyes. With a crackling voice they could hear Justin repeat repeatedly, "I'm sorry. I'm sorry." Justin continued this for almost three minutes before he broke into an uncontrollable sobbing.

CHAPTER XVII

THE CONFESSION

S ULLY GAVE JUSTIN ENOUGH TIME TO SINK INTO A
vulnerable state of depression until entering the room. Sully
walked into the room and threw down on the table several of the
gay magazines and DVD's that they had found at Justin's residence.

"It's clear you're queer!" Proclaimed Sully.

Justin, with his eyes completely teared up, said nothing. Sully
could clearly read the shame on Justin's face. More importantly, he
could see the fear in Justin's teary eyes.

"Justin. I'm a reasonable guy. All I want is for you to tell me
everything that you and your buddies did in Griffith Park. This
oddity that you have, this deep dark secret you have managed to
keep from your skinhead friends. Well, what do you say that we
keep it to ourselves? That would make you happy. I mean for your
buddies not to find out. Right?"

Justin answered sheepishly, "Yes sir."

Sully continued, "Okay, you make me happy and I'll make you
happy. So, let's get through the Miranda thing and well get down to
business."

Sully explained Justin's rights to him. Justin waived his right
to remain silent and agreed to talk to Sully without an attorney
present. Sully knew full well that he had all the evidence he needed
for a conviction of the skinheads. He really wasn't concerned that

a good defense attorney would be able to successfully challenge his Miranda waiver in court citing coercion and having Justin's statement held inadmissible. What Sully really wanted from Justin was evidence implicating Richard Reinstadt in the murders of Ralph Doyle and Amanda Cavanaugh.

Sully wanted to keep things in order, and he began with Elliot James Burton, the last victim first. Sully asked Justin to describe to him how they were able to coax Elliot into their car and what they intended to do to him. Justin explained that they were cruising Santa Monica Blvd. looking for a queer whore. Justin related that they saw Elliot on the sidewalk hooking so they stopped, engaged in conversation with him and reached a deal. Justin told the detective that Elliot agreed to party with all three of them for One Thousand Dollars.

Justin admitted that the skinheads had no intention of partying queer style with Elliot. Justin, with some reservation stated, "We were going to string him up between the trees at the top of the hill in Griffith Park. We would have beaten him just like the others. I would brand him as a fag for all to see. And, before he was dead, I would cut off his ear. It would be my own personal trophy."

"What about the dildo?" Sully pushed for more.

"To tell you the truth I don't remember just whose turn it was to shove the cock up his ass." Justin stated.

"So, let me get this straight. You guys took turns ramming the dildo up the ass of your prey?" Asked Sully.

"Yes sir." Justin responded.

Meg and Kathy Burgess were still in the other room. And, though the interview between Detective Sullivan and Justin Davis was being tape recorded, they were taking notes. This was being done because they would eventually interview Keith Thomas and Franklyn Andrews. They would want to show how Justin laid each one of them out for each of the Griffith Park murders. This would be the tactic used to solicit statements from each one of them. Lock them into a story before they clam up and ask for an attorney.

Sully then directed Justin to the previous victim, Gregory James Jefferson. Justin's eyes again began filling up with tears. Sully felt that Justin might be a little reluctant to relive the accounts of this murder. Especially if he were the one who used the vise grips to crush Gregory's testicles. To Sully's surprise Justin began to retell the events of that night. However, with tears and with what Sully felt was sincere remorse.

"It was before midnight on Friday," Justin began. "Keith Thomas, Franklyn Andrews and I were cruising Melrose Avenue when we saw the half white, half black fag come out of the gay bar. We followed him into the parking lot and jumped him. We pulled him into the car and drove him to Griffith Park. You know, up behind the water tank."

Sully questioned, "He didn't resist or yell out for help?"

"We put a hood over his head to muffle his screams," Justin answered. "He really didn't struggle until we took him out of the car. We had to drag him up the trail to the top of the hill. Once we were at the top of the hill, we stripped him of his clothes. Then we bound his hands and feet and drew him up between the trees, so his feet were off the ground. He started to yell out for help when we took the hood off of his head, so I taped his mouth shut."

Justin again began to hesitate. Sully knew it was nearing the point in the events where one of the skinheads tortured Gregory with the vise grips. Sully asked Justin if he was avoiding the vise grip usage on the victim's balls. Justin nodded and Sully asked, "Did you yourself use the vise grips on Gregory Jefferson?"

"No sir," Justin answered with a degree of shame. "It was Franklyn."

"Why? What reason would you guys have to mutilate that young man in that fashion?" Sully questioned.

"He was a half breed. We were purifying his blood so he could pass on as white." Justin explained.

"And the dildo?" Sully questioned, "Who shoved the dildo up his ass?"

"I'm not sure. I think it was Keith." Justin responded.

Meg and Kathy Burgess still taking notes paid attention to the statement that Keith Thomas was responsible for the dildo in the rectum of Gregory. As it would turn out after interviewing the other two skinheads, they would learn that it was in fact Justin who placed the rubber dick into the ass of Gregory. Justin too would admit to this act when his memory was refreshed.

Sully asked Justin about the ear. Justin told the Detective that he cut the ear off as a trophy. Justin admitted that he was the one that possessed all four ears. Justin related that each of the murders were almost the same. The victims were picked up near gay bars or streets where gays sell themselves for sexual acts. They were all taken to the hilltop in Griffith Park. They were then stripped naked and suspended in the trees.

Justin told Sully that each one of the queers was branded. He told the Detective that they had a small blow torch that he kept in the trunk of his car. They would heat the branding iron with the torch before burning it into the skin of the fag hanging in the tree. They would cram the dildo in their ass and then he would cut off the right ear. Justin then told Sully that the three would beat their victim until they were dead.

Justin's recollection was pretty good. He had forgotten that it was he who had jammed the huge dildo into the ass of Gregory and blamed Keith Thomas for the act. But, all in all, he was able to recite the details of the other three cases involving the murder of Gerald Clark, Richard Black and Peter Washington. After the three-hour interview had concluded, Sully was confident that as far as the four murders in Griffith Park were concerned, he had gotten all he could.

Sully was exhausted and it was clear to see that Justin too was spent. In fact, you could describe him more clearly if you were to say he was emotionally drained. It was time for a break Sully thought. Actually, his team was far ahead of him. Kathy Burgess had already made a quick trip to In and Out for some double doubles with grilled onions, some fries and chocolate shakes.

Sully had walked out of the room for a breather at the same time as Lieutenant Flemming escorted young Justin to the restroom for a head call. By the time Justin was returned to the Interrogation Room his double cheeseburger, fries and chocolate shake were there waiting for him.

Sully and his team sat outside at a table. It was a clear night in Hollywood. Warm, but not too hot. Sully lit up one of his Tronquitos from Leon's and puffed his way through this cigar while at the same time savoring his cuisine from In and Out. Sully was beyond satisfied with his interrogation of Justin thus far. However, he knew that the best had not been drawn out of Justin as yet.

The rest of Sully's team was elated as well. But yet they also knew that Sully still needed to address the murders of Amanda Cavanaugh and Detective Ralph Doyle. The team put together crime scene photos from the home of Ralph Doyle, as well as photos from the abandoned house in Bakersfield which was the site of the brutal murder of Amanda and, of course, there were the photographs of Richard Reinstadt. Both the team and Sully knew that they would need Justin to implicate Reinstadt in these murders.

Sully re-entered the Interview Room just as Justin was forcing the last drops of his milkshake through his straw.

Sully commented, "Sounds like that hit the spot Justin."

"Yeah. Thanks. It was good. I didn't know that I was that hungry." Justin answered.

"Are you ready to continue with this Justin?" Sully asked.

"Yes Sir. I am ready. I'd like to get it all out there and get it over with. You know what I mean? I just want to clear the air." Justin responded.

Sully wasn't sure how Justin would react when seeing the photographs of Amanda Cavanaugh. As far as Sully knew, Justin was still hung up on the killings up in Griffith Park. Sully then laid out a series of photographs taken of Amanda Cavanaugh in Bakersfield.

Justin's eyes began to tear up. It was clear that Sully hit a nerve that Justin didn't see coming.

"You want to tell me how you three pulled this off?" Sully asked. Sully knew instinctively that Justin, as well as Franklyn Andrews and Keith Thomas were present at Amanda's murder. He also felt strongly that all three took part in the murder of his friend, Ralph Doyle. But Sully knew down deep in his gut that Richard Reinstadt was behind the murders of Cavanaugh and Doyle. What he didn't know were the facts surrounding Reinstadt's part in the murders.

"We drove Amanda up to Bakersfield. We had been given the address of that abandoned house and we took her there," Justin began.

"Who gave you your marching orders? Who told you to bring Amanda to that house?" Sully asked.

"Richard." Justin stated.

Sully waited for Justin to fill in the blanks. However, after a prolonged pause, it was clear that Justin had hit a stalling point; most likely out of fear.

"Richard Reinstadt? Is that who gave you your instructions?" Sully prodded.

"Yes. Yes Sir. It was Richard Reinstadt. He told us that she was a rat and that she had been talking to ZOG. Richard told us to pick her up and bring her to him in Bakersfield." Justin conceded.

Sully stopped the questioning momentarily. He wanted to calm Justin a little. It was apparent that introducing Richard Reinstadt had brought with it some uneasy feelings in Justin. Sully surmised that Reinstadt had some type of hold on the Skinheads. Most likely there was a shared respect as well as fear that they held for Reinstadt.

Justin took a couple of deep breaths, looked at Sully and assured him that he was fine. Justin related that he, along with Franklyn and Keith had picked Amanda up on a Friday morning. They had driven up the coast to Pismo Beach. Justin told Sully that the four of them spent the day digging for clams.

It was almost dark when they left the beach. Justin told Sully that they drove down to Santa Maria on the Coast Highway and then cut off on Taft Road. Justin related that they took this road all the way to Bakersfield. The only stop they made was in Taft, where they stopped to use the bathroom and buy a bottle of wine. The wine, according to Justin, was Reinstadt's idea. He wanted Amanda intoxicated by the time they reached the house in Bakersfield.

Justin was talking rather rapidly, and Sully was glad this was all on tape. The team in the next room monitoring the interview was also glad Justin's account of the events were being taped. They too were having a hard time keeping up with their note taking. Well, Kathy and Meg anyway. Anthony Flemming didn't take notes.

Sully interrupted Justin, "Why don't we take it from when you took Amanda into the house to meet Richard Reinstadt, shall we?"

Justin began, "We pulled up into the driveway and turned off the engine. But I left the headlights on. Then we got the all clear.

Richard flashed a light out of the window. Amanda, she didn't know from nothing. She was drunk from the wine. She probably thought we were all going to fuck her or something."

"So, you did get her drunk with the wine then?" Asked Sully.

"Oh yeah. She was drunk on her ass. Or, at least that's how it looked up until she saw Richard." Justin added, "When she saw Richard standing in the empty room she went into a panic and tried to pull away. I think she thought she could just run off."

Sully again stopped Justin. "Okay Justin. I want you to really think about what happened in the house step-by-step. And tell us who did what. Just like Griffith Park. Give me exactly what happened in a chronological order, Okay?"

"Sure. I understand. You want me to take it slow. Not to skip around. You want a play-by-play, so to speak." Justin interrupted.

"We grabbed Amanda. Me, Franklyn and Keith. We tied her wrists and ankles just like we did with the queers in the park. We stretched her out and suspended her in air between the posts. Then we stood back and watched Richard go to work on her. At first, he didn't say anything to her. He just took out his big ass knife and slowly began cutting her clothing off until she was buck naked. Richard put his mouth over one of her nipples and began to suck hard on it. At the same time, he reached up, with his right hand, between her legs. I think he put his finger into her. Then all of a sudden he jumped back and started talking to her."

"You have been talking to 'ZOG!' You have betrayed your race and must be cleansed of your sins!"

"No, no you've got it all wrong! I would never turn on my Aryan people!" Amanda cried out with a notable tone of fear in her voice.

Justin told Sully that Reinstadt continued to argue with her telling Amanda that he knew for a fact that she was in bed with the enemy "ZOG" and that she must confess her sinful deeds to him. Reinstadt then took out his lighter.

"Amanda was suspended there in mid air with her legs spread way apart." Justin began to explain. "Reinstadt took the flame of his lighter and passed it back and forth between her legs over her girl parts. The flame was touching her. I know it was. You could see her flinch. It would have singed all her hair off down there except

145

for the fact that Amanda kept herself shaved. She braved it out man. She never cried out."

Justin paused and Sully thought Justin was starting to falter a bit, so he offered to get Justin some water. Justin looked at Sully and smiled. It was as if Justin had found a friend that understood his troubles.

"Coffee. I would like coffee. Hot and black. If that's Okay. That's what I would like."

Sully nodded his head in agreement. "You know Justin, coffee sounds good. I could use a cup of the black stuff myself."

Sully stood and opened the door. Lieutenant Flemming was already standing on the other side holding two cups of hot, black coffee. Sully returned to the table and the two began to slowly sip on the brew. Sully could see that this was time well spent. Justin was becoming more relaxed. More importantly, he was becoming more comfortable with Sully. This would make it easier for him to speak of the horrid details of Amanda's murder.

Justin took a couple of sips of coffee and began once again to tell Sully exactly what took place in the house in Bakersfield.

"Well. I'm sure the flame of the lighter was hot, especially on Amanda's girl stuff. But you know, I don't think she got burned. I don't know, maybe her stuff was too wet to burn, or Richard just passed the flame by too fast. It seemed like it was taking forever. Richard was toying with her. What a sadistic son of a bitch! Then he stopped. Richard just put his lighter into his pocket. He looked at her and he said, "You're going to tell me who it is you've been talking to. You ratted out your brothers and sisters in the Guardians. You will tell me the name of 'ZOG.'"

"This is what Reinstadt said to Amanda?" Asked Sully.

"Yes sir. Then when she wouldn't answer him, he began sucking on her nipples to make them hard. But she was so afraid that he got no reaction. Richard then grabbed a sixteen-ounce container of coke, well it was empty, except the ice cubes. Richard took the top off and tiled the container up and filled his mouth with ice. Richard then placed his mouth filled with ice over Amanda's right tit. The nipple reacted to the ice. It got really hard. Richard took a pair of vise grips and clamped onto the nipple. He tightened down until

Amanda groaned in pain. She just kinda moaned under her breath. She still would not scream out. I think this pissed Richard off. I really believe he wanted to hear her cry out in agony or something."

"You're doing just fine Justin. You need a little time? Maybe have another sip of your coffee?" Sully suggested.

"No. I'm okay sir." Justin did take another gulp of his coffee which had now cooled down just a tad. "Richard put more ice in his mouth and grabbed Amanda's left tit. He engulfed it with his ice filled mouth. The reaction was again the same. Amanda's nipple hardened and stuck straight out. Richard took a second pair of vise grips and tightened down on this nipple as well. Richard stepped back and stood about three feet in front of Amanda. The conversation went something like this."

Richard: "You're going to tell me exactly what I want to know and what I want to know is the name of the cop or the Fed that you have been talking to."

Amanda: "You're crazy. I haven't talked to anyone about my friends!"

Justin explained, "I think that was the wrong answer because Richard turned the knob tightening the vise grip on Amanda's right nipple. Then he began talking softly to Amanda."

Richard: "That is not the answer I had in mind. You have betrayed your race and you are going to confess your sins. You can scream out all you want but there is no one around to hear you."

Amanda: "I don't know what you want me to say. I have done nothing wrong!"

"Reinstadt began to tighten the vise grips altering left and right. He tightened them to the point where he began to draw blood from Amanda's right nipple. Amanda was crying at this point. Yet she still did not cry out." Justin stated.

Justin then explained that Reinstadt was becoming angry. Enraged as Justin put it. He was beside himself. He had inflicted more pain that is humanly possible to stand. According to Justin, Reinstadt grabbed a set of bolt cutters. He told Justin to grab Amanda's right hand and hold her index finger out.

Justin, now in tears, begged Sully to believe him.

"I couldn't do it to her. Please. You have got to believe me. I couldn't. Even though Richard had put the fear in me. He called me a queer baby and yelled for me to grab her hand. But I couldn't do it sir. I couldn't."

"I believe you Justin. You were right to refuse," assured Sully.

"Franklyn, that piece of shit suck ass Franklyn, he grabbed her hand and jerked her index finger straight out for Richard to cut off," explained Justin.

According to Justin, Richard then held the finger up to Amanda's face. He accused her of using the finger to point ZOG in the direction of the Guardians of Israel. It wasn't until Reinstadt threatened Amanda with the bolt cutters once again that she began to talk. Reinstadt ran the blade of the bolt cutters up and down over her vise grip pinched nipples. He promised to snip them off if she didn't confess her sins.

Amanda was now sobbing, both from the pain inflicted upon her and the fact that she would now name Detective Ralph Doyle as the one she had been talking to. It wasn't so much that she would be betraying Ralph's trust, it was that she was truly in love with Doyle. She found security in his arms. This was a man she looked up to. Kind of a father figure but, at the same time, just an older man that fulfilled her needs and not just sexually, he also offered her guidance.

Justin continued to explain in detail what had happened to Amanda. He told Sully that Amanda told Richard that she had been working with the LAPD, a Detective named Doyle. Richard thanked Amanda for her candor. Richard left the room just for a moment and returned with a red-hot fireplace poker. Justin related that he later learned that Reinstadt had a hibachi in the kitchen. He had been heating up the poker as well as a branding iron.

"Richard walked back into the room with the poker. It was bright red; it was so hot. He told Amanda that she did not deserve to wear the badges of honor that she had placed on her body. He burned her. He just melted her flesh removing her Swastika and lightning bolts. Then he simply walked out of the room. He came back into the room in a matter of seconds. This time he had a Star of David branding iron. Richard burned a Star of David into Amanda's chest. He told her that she would be forever more branded a Race Traitor!"

"What happened next? How was she killed?" Sully asked.

"Richard told us to beat the shit out of her. I couldn't do it. I liked Amanda. I couldn't hit her." Justin replied.

"You know Justin? There is one thing I don't understand." Sully stated.

"What's that?" Justin asked.

"Well. We had been told that you and Amanda had been boyfriend-girlfriend." Sully added.

"I see. Because I'm queer you don't understand about me and Amanda." Replied Justin.

"Yes. I admit it. I'm confused." Sully questioned.

"Look. I tried going straight. Believe me I wanted to be a normal pussy fucking guy. Every chick that wanted in with the Guardians had to fuck me. I really was trying to find the girl that could get me off. And, they loved it. I could go for an hour. No sweat. I just could shoot my load. I mean the girls loved it. They were crying out in total ecstasy. Pussy just didn't do it for me. A big cock though would get me off in the blink of an eye." Justin explained.

Justin went on to tell Sully that Franklyn Andrews, Keith Thomas and occasionally Richard punched Amanda until she was unconscious. Then Keith continued to punch her in the stomach.

"I'm sure I saw blood coming out of the corner of her mouth." Added Justin.

According to Justin, Richard Reinstadt stepped in and stopped Keith Thomas from hitting Amanda further. In fact, Reinstadt felt for a pulse in Amanda's neck but failed to find any sign of life. Reinstadt told the Skinheads that the Race Traitor bitch was dead.

He told the boys to head back to Los Angeles and that he would clean things up.

"We left her there. Her battered body just hanging there limp-like. She was my friend." Justin remarked while tears welled up in the corner of his eyes.

Sully knew it was time for another break. He had Lieutenant Flemming take Justin down the hall for a head call. Sully fixed them both another cup of coffee. It was time to talk about the murder of Ralph Doyle. Sully was a little apprehensive. He felt that Justin would freeze up when it came to reliving the murder of a cop.

Justin re-entered the room refreshed. He saw the coffee there for him and his eyes lit up. Justin drank the coffee and sighed.

"Now that hit the spot. Only trouble is, I'll probably need to pee again." Justin remarked.

Sully laid out some crime scene photographs from Doyle's house. Justin didn't show any signs of shock or fear. He went right into it.

"That's the cop Amanda was working with. Richard found him and so we waited in the bushes for him to come home. He was really drunk. Good thing for us or he would have kicked our asses. This old cop was strong as an ox. He put up a good fight, but we finally wore him down. Now we didn't do anything to the cop. Oh, yeah, we tied him up and all. We stretched him out in the air like we did Amanda, but we didn't do anything else. Richard was the only one that hurt him." Justin claimed.

As it turned out, Justin, Franklyn and Keith didn't witness Reinstadt brutalizing Doyle. They had left before Reinstadt tortured Doyle. Before the branding and before Reinstadt removed Doyle's right index finger. But what Justin did have to offer was Richard Reinstadt as the murder suspect.

"Richard told me to get his bag out of the trunk of his car. I went out to the car and got this black leather bag out of the trunk. It was like one of those old doctor's bags. You know, like in those old movies when the doctor makes house calls. Anyway, Richard opened the bag and he took out his syringe. He told the cop that he was going to give him a shot that would boil his blood and then he would be dead. He injected the cop in the ass. You know he was naked. I mean, when I came back into the house the cop didn't have any clothes on. I guess Richard, Franklyn and Keith stripped him down when I went to the car."

"You didn't see anything after Reinstadt gave him the shot?" Sully asked.

"No. He told us to leave. But I could see that whatever Richard gave him was taking effect. His eyes were rolling back into his head. We did what we were told. We left. I drove Keith and Andrew home and then I went home myself." Justin concluded.

CHAPTER XVIII

BLACK POWDER

ULLY HAD COMPLETED HIS INTERROGATION OF Justin. It would now be up to Kathy Burgess, Meg and Lieutenant Flemming to sit down with Franklyn Andrews and Keith Thomas to deliver the bad news. Hopefully, the two of them would then open up and present their side of what had taken place at the six homicides.

Sully walked out of the interrogation room and to his surprise found Captain Stephanie Porter standing on the other side of the door. The Captain congratulated Sully on a job well done. Sully had not known that Captain Porter had been listening to the interrogation of Justin as it pertained to the murders of Amanda Cavanaugh and Detective Ralph Doyle.

"Detective Sullivan," Captain Porter began, "I have a Detective III position open at Robbery Homicide Division. The new deployment period begins two weeks from today and I need to fill the position. I want your application for the job on my desk tomorrow morning. See you then."

Captain Porter turned and walked away. She never gave Sully the opportunity to respond. Sully knew that if Stephanie Porter was telling him to apply then she wanted him for the spot. A Captain isn't going to basically order you to apply for a promotional position in his or her command if they don't intend for you to have the job.

Sully was a Detective II, which is the equivalent to a Field Sergeant. A Detective III is a huge step not only in status but in pay as well. Sully loved working Homicide, and he especially loved working it at Newton Street. But Sully knew that at Newton Street promoting to Detective III was about five years away. And, even then, he would be competing against other Detectives with greater seniority in Homicide. No, Sully knew that this was his shot at promoting and that this promotion would greatly benefit himself and his family financially.

Sully would begin working on his paperwork for submittal to Captain Porter. But first he needed to reach out to Special Agent Penny Adler. Agent Adler would need to be briefed on Justin's confession as it related to the murders of Cavanaugh and Doyle. She would need to know that it was Richard Reinstadt who actually planned and executed the murders.

"Penny? This is Sully. I have some good news for you."

"Good Sully. I have some juicy stuff for you too. But why don't you go first." Agent Adler responded.

"Justin Davis opened up big time. He acknowledged that he, along with Franklyn Andrews and Keith Thomas killed the homo's in Griffith Park. Better yet, he admitted that he and his buddies drove Amanda Cavanaugh up to Bakersfield to meet Richard Reinstadt at that abandoned home. Justin told us that it was Reinstadt that tortured Amanda and got her to tell him all about Doyle. Reinstadt burned her body and it was Reinstadt that cut of her finger."

Agent Adler interrupted, "Damn Sully. Then Reinstadt must have both Amanda's, as well as Ralph's fingers at his apartment."

"That would be my guess too," acknowledged Sully. "Amanda was then beaten to death by the Skinheads. Reinstadt planned the murder of Doyle using the Skinheads as muscle. Reinstadt was responsible for the physical abuses done to Doyle including the amputation of his finger. It was also Reinstadt who injected Ricin into his system.

Agent Adler told Sully that she would incorporate all of that into her Search Warrant. Penny told Sully in response to his inquiry as to how things were going with the Warrant.

"While you were beating a confession out of Justin, we had some real progress with Reinstadt as well."

"What do you mean beat a confession out of my suspect?" Sully questioned.

"Come on Sully. We, at the FBI, know that beating confessions out of suspects is a six-hour class at the LAPD Police Academy," Penny laughed.

"Two hours," Sully quipped. "It's a two-hour class and we have to furnish our own rubber hose."

After the mutual laughter subsided Agent Adler informed Sully that the Bureau's Surveillance Team had taken Reinstadt on another shopping spree. This time Reinstadt visited the Big Five in Vista. There he purchased eight pounds of smokeless black powder. Penny assured Sully that the United States Attorney would file on Reinstadt for possession of explosive devices at the very least. Penny advised that it was the opinion of the Justice Department. That so long as Reinstadt had the following components in the same area or close proximity they would consider him to possess a device. The components were pipes, end caps, gunpowder and some type of initiator. Penny advised Sully that she had explained to the U.S. Attorney that they did have Reinstadt purchasing thermostats that contained mercury switches. She added that when she explained the bombing at this residence, the one that killed U.S. Postal Carrier Michael Sanders, and the fact that a mercury switch was used in that device, her Search Warrant was in the bag.

Agent Adler told Sully that they would hit Reinstadt's apartment at 7:00 a.m. in the morning. She told Sully that under the items to be seized in the search she would include human index fingers.

"Sully. Did you want to come out and play in the morning? You'd only have to be in Fallbrook at 6:00 a.m. for briefing." Agent Adler offered an invitation to Sully to take part in the search.

"No. I would like to be, but I've got to type up Justin's confession. And, I've got to have my request for transfer on Stephanie Porter's desk in the morning as well," Sully explained.

"Transfer? Where are you going?" Penny questioned.

"Captain Porter has offered me a shot at a Detective III position at Robbery-Homicide Division," he told her.

"Take it!" Penny exclaimed. "Take it. God knows you deserve it! I'll call you after the search with the details." She assured him.

It would be late into the evening when Sully completed his reports detailing his interview of Justin. The reports were broken into six separate confessions so that the details of one homicide did not contaminate the details of another. After completing his reports on Justin's confession, he sat down to assist his team with their reports. Kathy Burgess, Lieutenant Flemming, as well as Meg, had been able to obtain confessions from both Andrews and Thomas as well. The two boys told the investigators exactly what they had done. They also told them exactly what Justin had done. They were a little reluctant to talk about Richard Reinstadt. However, if they were told what Justin Davis had said about Reinstadt they both would open up and confirm what Justin had said. They would not, however, offer up any information on Reinstadt on their own.

After Sully saw that his team had everything under control, he filled out the paperwork that Captain Porter had requested. It was almost 11:00 p.m. when Sully took Meg by the hand and walked her out to the parking lot. It was past time to go home and it was now the right time to tell Meg about the offer that Stephanie Porter had made.

"Meg," Sully stopped in his tracts.

"Yes Sully. What is it?" She questioned.

"Captain Porter has offered me a Detective III spot at Robbery-Homicide Division." Sully told her.

"D-III! Isn't that about a Lieutenant's pay?" She asked.

"Close. Not quite, but pretty close. At least after a year in grade." He explained.

"You would have to leave Newton," she expressed sadly. "Could you do that?" She questioned.

"Yeah. I think I could. Oh, it would be tough to leave the guys at Newton, but you know this would be good for my career. Heck, this would be good for us!" He justified.

"Then, do it Sully. If she wants you then she must think very highly of you. You should go for it." Meg assured.

It was six o'clock in the morning when Special Agent Penny Adler met with her FBI search team. This Monday morning, in the

North San Diego County, was socked in with heavy fog. This would keep the air unit grounded. This proved to be very unfortunate for the FBI. Because of the lack of air cover, Reinstadt would be able to elude the FBI.

The one thing that Agent Adler did not know about her nemesis was that Reinstadt did have a small camera mounted on the face of the apartment complex. This camera projected the parking lot activities onto a monitor in Reinstadt's apartment. So, when the first agents appeared in the parking area of Reinstadt's complex, he was forewarned.

Reinstadt had not lived in this complex for more than nine to ten weeks. Not long by most standards. However, long enough to assure himself an escape route. Located in the bathroom over his toilet was an attic crawl space. Reinstadt's apartment was located on the second floor at the extreme east end of the apartment structure. This structure was slightly longer than a football field. At the west end of the flat roof building was another apartment building in the complex. This structure was identical to Reinstadt's building. However, it sat down on a terraced lot which gave it a ten-foot drop from the unit Reinstadt occupied. There was also about a seven-foot spread between the two buildings.

Although Reinstadt had not been a resident of the complex for a long period of time, he was able to make a few modifications without being detected. The first thing he did was to mount a security camera on the roof above his apartment. In preparation for an evacuation route, Reinstadt began cutting a passage door in each of the firewalls. He would need only to disguise the first passageway to mask his escape.

At the west end of the apartment building was a common stairwell. Not only was there an access door in the stairwell that led into the attic, there was an access door to the roof. Reinstadt was confident that he could make a running jump down onto the roof top of the next apartment building in the complex. He could then run down that roof top to the stairwell on the opposite end and complete his escape.

As it turned out, all of his pre-planning paid off. It was 6:45 a.m. when Reinstadt observed the images on his monitor: Agents in

FBI raid jackets armed with what appeared to be MP-Five assault weapons. Reinstadt deactivated the camera and turned the monitor to a regular television. He didn't want them to see that he had been monitoring the parking lot. He wanted the FBI to believe that he had not been at home when they came knocking. This would ease his efforts to escape.

Reinstadt made his way into the attic and closed his crawl space. He made his way through the first firewall and replaced the section of cut out wall giving the appearance that the wall was complete. He made his way to the end of the attic. There, he had a change of clothes and three weapons. The first of which was a 9mm Smith and Wesson which he tucked into his lower back with the assistance of a soft inside holster. The secondhand gun was a Browning 25 semi-automatic which he placed into his right front pant's pocket. Reinstadt left the third weapon, an AR-15 fully automatic, in the attic.

Reinstadt made his way to the roof. Under normal circumstances he would have immediately been spotted by a law enforcement helicopter which would have accompanied the FBI search team. However, things don't always go as planned. This Monday morning, fog grounded the helicopter. Reinstadt got a running start and jumped from his building to the next. He made his way to the stairwell at the far end and made good his escape.

It was at 7:00 a.m. when the FBI did its knock and notice. They banged with four successive wall rattling raps to the door while yelling out, "FBI. We have a search warrant!" After a moment, with no response, the entry team kicked the door open.

After clearing the apartment, including a look at the attic, the FBI concluded that Reinstadt had left during the night. They began their search, although the definition of the work search really did not fit in. On the kitchen table the FBI found, right out there for the world to see, three explosive devices. The pipes, or nipples as they are called, were twelve inches in length and two inches in diameter. They were filled with smokeless black powder with the end caps attached. A small hole had been drilled into the end of one end cap on each device. Inserted into the gunpowder was a blasting cap. The blasting cap was attached to wires that had been fed through the hole in the end cap. Those wires were attached to a nine-volt battery taped to the pipe. One of the wires was severed with an end attached to a mercury switch. The other end lay unattached.

The San Diego Sheriffs Department Bomb Squad was called in to render the three devices safe. In the interim, the Agents stopped their search of Reinstadt's apartment and assisted Sheriff's Deputies with the evacuation of the apartment building.

It was 10:00 o'clock when the agents once again began their search. Agent Penny Adler diverted her focus from the search to the explosive devices. With her was L.A.P.D. Bomb Tech Jody Feder's report on the device used at the Sullivan residence. Penny presented the report to the San Diego bomb techs. They were able to dismantle one of the devices safely. After making a comparison, they informed Agent Adler that the devices were basically the same. They were constructed in the same manner utilizing the same materials. The only difference was that these devices were using blasting caps as an initiator; while the device that killed the Postal Carrier had used a flash bulb.

The search inside continued. On the table, where the devices had been located, were three sheets of paper with names, addresses, and directions written on them. They were the homes of FBI Agent Penny Adler, LAPD Lieutenant Anthony Flemming, and the last one was for the Holocaust Museum in Los Angeles.

Penny Adler had just entered the apartment when her co-workers were reading over the directions to her residence. The team looked up and saw her standing there somewhat stunned. They acknowledged that she was a target of one of the explosive devices.

"Has anyone checked the freezer yet?" Penny asked as if not being disturbed by the news.

She was told that the freezer had not yet been searched. Penny walked over to the refrigerator. The freezer was a separate compartment atop the refrigerator. She opened the freezer door expecting to see it full of frozen dinners and possibly frozen vegetables. She was confident that after digging through all the foot items she would find the fingers she sought; most likely wrapped in foil and placed in a freezer bag. To her amazement, when she opened the door, the freezer was void of food. Not even an ice tray sat in the box. Out in plain sight, not wrapped in foil, not even in a plastic bag, were the two fingers lying on the shelf.

The search of Reinstadt's apartment proved worthy. The three explosive devices would tie him to the bombing at Sullivan's residence and the murder of U.S. Postal Carrier Michael Sanders. The recovery of the two right index fingers would link him to the murders of Ralph Doyle and Amanda Cavanaugh. In addition, Agents found telephone toll records in the form of bills which noted several phones from Reinstadt's residence to the phone number of Justin Davis.

Reinstadt had managed to elude capture on this Monday morning. But, by weeks end, he would be added to the FBI's Top Ten Most Wanted List.

CHAPTER XIX

ROBBERY-HOMICIDE

TWO WEEKS HAD PASSED, AND IT WAS NOW THE FIRST Monday morning of the new deployment period. Detective III William Sullivan reported to work at his new assignment. Kathy Burgess latched onto his arm and led him around making all the necessary introductions; a task that took the better part of his first hour at Robbery-Homicide Division.

At 8:00 a.m. Sully sat down with Kathy and a handful of other Detectives in the coffee room for his first morning cup of coffee. Kathy and the other Detectives would be his team. He would be their Supervisor.

What Sully and the others did not know was that several hundred miles away, in Hyder, Arizona, Richard Reinstadt had just sat down to breakfast at Denny's Coffee Shop. Reinstadt had managed to keep to himself; kind of coasting along without drawing attention to himself.

Reinstadt had just been served his Grand Slam breakfast and cut into his pancakes when the hostess began to seat a guest in the booth next to him: a young black man in his early twenties and his beautiful blond, blue-eyed wife, along with their 6 month old half-white, half-black baby.

Reinstadt went ballistic. He jumped up, grabbed his Grand Slam and threw it across the room and into a plate-glass window.

"Get this Nigger, his white whore and their mutant bastard away from me!" He yelled out.

Reinstadt's actions put the entire restaurant into shock. Everyone was so taken by this that they were powerless to react, much less respond. In fact, only one may have reacted. Perhaps it was because of his inability to really analyze what had happened.

Bruce Gatton was a big man, standing at six foot, two inches and weighing in at 260 pounds. He was a formidable character with his shaved head and reddish goatee. Bruce had grown up driving cattle on his Daddy's Arizona ranch. He had joined the United States Marine Corps at the age of eighteen and was deployed in combat during Desert Storm. Bruce was wounded in combat, but the gunshot is not what caused his disability. It was the mental stress of war; witnessing his buddies being killed in such horrific ways.

Although Bruce was diagnosed with psychological trauma, causing brain dysfunction, Bruce was as gentle and peaceful as could be. He was like an overgrown kid. But there was something in him that drove him to protect the little guy. The underdog, if you will.

When Bruce saw Reinstadt yelling at the couple and their baby, he walked over and grabbed Reinstadt by the arm. Bruce towered over the shorter man.

"You should behave yourself! These nice people didn't do you any wrong!"

Reinstadt said nothing in response. For everyone else at the Denny's Coffee Shop that day, it was clear that Reinstadt was scared to death of the bigger man. Reinstadt's silence gave Bruce cause to believe that Reinstadt would apologize to the young family and all would be right again. Bruce turned away and started back toward his booth. Reinstadt grabbed the wooden highchair they had brought over for the infant. He swung it with all his might shattering the chair over the back of the bigger man.

Bruce was somewhat stunned by the blow to the back, but he was not knocked down. Nor did he lose his balance. He simply turned around and grunted. Bruce charged at Reinstadt. He grabbed the little man, lifting him up, off of the floor. Bruce then propelled Reinstadt like a rocket right through the plate glass window.

Reinstadt laid on the walkway in front of the coffee shop. Reinstadt sustained numerous lacerations. Several of which were bone deep. Reinstadt, bleeding profusely, could not speak. One witness described his final noisy breaths as that of someone sucking the final drops of a milk shake through a straw.

It was 10:00 a.m. when Penny Adler called Sully with the news of Reinstadt's demise. The news, in itself, was actually a relief. No more Reinstadt running free meant no more worries about finding a bomb attached to your front door. This is news that he would hare with Meg first and then with Lieutenant Flemming.

Sully was able to locate Flemming at Newton Street. He was holding roll call for his gang unit.

"Lieutenant. Sir, its Sully. I thought you would like to know that Richard Reinstadt died this morning in Hyder, Arizona."

"Painful, I would hope." Replied Flemming.

Sully provided the Lieutenant with every detail right down to his gurgling last breath.

"That's good Sully. Thanks. You have done a good job. I know that Ralph would be proud that you were the one that nabbed his murderers. It's been my pleasure to have worked with you. And now that we have this wrapped up, I think I'll go ahead and submit my retirement papers today." Flemming admonished.

"Lieutenant. The Department will be losing an institution when you walk out the door." Sully finished.

Captain Porter entered the room and announced to Sully's team that the Housekeeping at the Bonaventure Hotel discovered three bodies in one of their suites with gunshots to the head. She added that Central Division Detectives made the initial entry. They say it looks like a mob hit and would like us to take it off their hands.

"Welcome to Robbery Homicide Detective Sullivan. Your team is up." Added Captain Porter.

It was 12:15 in the afternoon when Sully and his team arrived at the Bonaventure. They were led up to a suite on the twentieth floor by Sergeant Bryan Anderson. As they entered the suite, they found the three men, all Caucasian, were lying face down on the floor. They were dressed in suits. Not just business suits. These were not off the rack J.C. Penney suits. These were C.E.O. type attire.

The men's' hands were bound behind their backs with duct tape. Their ankles were also taped together. Duct tape was used to secure their hands together with their feet preventing them from moving around. A single strand of duct tape was placed over their mouths.

Each man was shot execution style in the back of the head, mob style. Sully had the eerie feeling that this was made to look like a mob hit but felt otherwise. Sully found a pillow with gun powder burns on it. Sully believed that the pillow was used to muffle the guns shots. Sully thought to himself that if this was a mob hit, a professional hit man would have used a silencer.

The person or persons responsible for this were not mob hit men. They left too much evidence behind. Sully noted hair follicles stuck to the duct tape. A hit man would have shaved the hair off his arms and knuckles to avoid such a blunder.

Kathy Burgers had been examining the three briefcases in the room. All three had been pried open and ransacked. Kathy believed that a knife had been used to jimmy the cases open. She found blood on one cases indicating that one of the suspects had cut himself prying open the briefcase.

The team turned its attention to the briefcases in an effort to identify the three victims. The first briefcase had the initials G.E.B. on the top under the handle. Paperwork inside had the name of George Edward Bishop Jr., Vice President on Chase Manhattan Bank letterhead. The second case had the name Preston located under the handle as well. Inside this case the Detectives found documents identifying Allen Alexander Preston, Projects Engineeer, for Exxon-Mobil Oil Company. The third briefcase had no name or initials on the exterior. However, inside the briefcase was an identification card issued by the United States Department of the Interior. The card was issued to Jonathan T. Pickford, Assistant to the Secretary of the Interior.

Sully looked at his team and stated, "What we have here is a Corporate Conspiracy!"

Printed in the United States
By Bookmasters